RED DIRT HEART CHRISTMAS

BONUS STORY : RED DIRT HEART IMAGO

N.R. WALKER

COPYRIGHT

DEDICATION

For all my readers, who encourage me to keep writing. Your emails and messages of support are the highlight of my day.

To Sam Higson, for planting this little plot-bunny seed.
To Robyn, for helping with Brennan's name.
To Nic, for helping with the right photo.

I hope you all enjoy this short trip with old friends...

N.R. WALKER

Red DIRT HEART Christmas

RED DIRT HEART CHRISTMAS

BLURB

Travis had been here at Sutton Station for just over a year. We were technically engaged, not that we'd told anyone. He was happy just knowin' I'd said yes, and I had some head-clearin' stuff to work through. Knowing I was good enough for Trav was one thing, but knowing if I was good enough to be a husband and father was somethin' else entirely.

Life at Sutton Station had never been better. Business was strong, Trudy and Bacon's little baby, Gracie, was a few weeks old now and as cute as a button, Ma's health was good, and my relationship with Laura and Sam was in a pretty good place. And Travis? Well, life with him was still all kinds of perfect.

But, to Travis's dismay, Christmas at the Station was just another day. Another day of getting up before the sun, feeding animals, fixin' what needed fixin', and checking water troughs all while tryin' to keep out of the blistering heat.

And this year weren't much different. Only that it was Travis's first Sutton Station Christmas. The fact we didn't go all out with decorations and celebrations baffled him, and if I was bein' truthful, it disappointed him too.

Which was why I had to make it a special kind of Christmas...

DEDICATION

For everyone who has read the Red Dirt Heart series and loved these boys as much as me, may your Christmases be filled with love and happiness. And toe-bitin' wombats, Outback tinsel that bleeds, and a whole lotta red, red dirt.

NOTE FROM THE AUTHOR:

This book uses Australian English spelling and grammar.
There will be words like brumbies (wild horses) Macca's
(McDonald's) and a serious lack of g's on most ing words.
There are also run-on hyphenated sentences. It's just how
Charlie speaks.

TIMELINE ACKNOWLEDGMENT:

Anyone familiar with the Red Dirt Heart series will know it spans the seasons. In RDH1 when Travis arrives, it's summer, RDH2 is autumn/winter, RDH3 is spring and RDH4, being Trav's pov, is back to summer and spans another year. Christmas in Australia is in summer, so according to the actual timeline of the series, Travis' first Christmas falls between RDH3 and RDH4, though it is not mentioned.

So, like a small snippet of something that didn't technically happen, this Christmas story is of Travis' first Christmas at Sutton Station, therefore falls between books 3 and 4.

They're not married, there's no Milly.

A small reminder of where the storyline was up to… Travis has asked Charlie to marry him, but they've not told anyone yet. Trudy and Bacon have just had their first baby, Gracie, and Nugget still steals every scene he's in.

Enjoy.

IT'S BEGINNING TO LOOK A LOT LIKE
CHRISTMAS

I WAS MUCKIN' out the stables with Billy when he stopped and leaned on his shovel. He was lookin' out to the paddock and grinned his half-a-face smile. "Ah, boss. You might wanna take a look."

I followed his line of sight and let out a long sufferin' sigh. "Jesus."

Billy laughed and I shook my head. We could see Trav smilin' as he rode the dirt bike into the yard. Strapped onto the seat behind him was a six foot pine tree. He pulled the bike to a stop, and his grin got even wider.

I stared at him. "Trav, what's that?"

"What does it look like?" he asked, his eyebrows knitting together. "It's a tree."

"I can see that."

"Mr Travis," Billy said, all concerned-like. "You can't be cuttin' them trees down. They special to the Aboriginal people's culture. Mr Travis, you disrespectin' our people."

Travis's face was priceless. He paled, his eyes went wide, and his mouth fell open. He looked at me for some kind of guidance, and I just shook my head and clicked my tongue. Travis turned back to Billy, close to panicking. "Oh. I didn't know. Oh my God. I just thought it looked like a Christmas tree and there were plenty of them. Billy, I'm so sorry. I can take it back. I mean, I can't replant it 'cause you know." He looked at the tree on the back of the bike and cringed. "Well, I hacked it off at the ground. God, I'm so sorry. Is there something I should do?"

Billy looked at the tree. "Well, there's a spirit dance from the Dreamtime. The person who takes the tree needs to do it."

Travis nodded seriously. "A spirit dance?"

Trav stared at Billy, and I stared at Billy. *A spirit dance?* I had to give it to Billy. He held it together for about five seconds of absolute silence before he lost it. He burst out laughing, which made me laugh too. "I'm just pullin' your leg, Travis. There's no spirit dance," Billy said, holding his sides as he laughed. His smile was so contagious.

Apparently Travis was immune. He glared at us. "Oh, you sons of bitches. You had me going." He put his hand to his heart. "Jesus Billy, you scared the crap outta me. I thought I'd broken some traditional Aboriginal code or something!"

Billy just laughed some more. "The look on your face was so funny."

"I hate the both of you," Trav said, but he was smiling.

"These trees are like a weed," Billy said. "Introduced by the white fellas two hundred years ago. They grow fast, but they're not native."

"I didn't think they were." Travis ran his hand along the fronds of the tethered tree. "But it's the closest thing to a Christmas tree out here."

"Christmas tree?" Billy asked. "Not too old for that? Still think Santa Claus climbs down chimneys?"

Travis frowned. He looked at his feet and shifted his weight. His voice was quiet. "No. It was just a tradition in my family. My grandfather would cut down a tree and we'd decorate it as a family. We had special ornaments and there would be a huge dinner and it was kind of a big deal. I just thought maybe... You know what? Never mind."

Billy knew Travis's grandfather had died not long ago. "Oh Mr Travis, I didn't mean anything. I was just jokin' with ya. Here, let me help you get it off the bike."

Travis sighed and his frowned deepened, and Billy quickly undid the straps and lifted the tree by himself. "Where do you want it, Mr Travis?"

Trav was lookin' down at the dirt, and Billy stared at me with wide eyes. "Boss? I didn't mean nothin' by it," he whispered.

I saw the corner of Travis's lip curl up and I rolled my eyes. "Oh, for shit's sake. He's joking, Billy."

Billy's eyes shot to Travis, and Travis's frown became a slow spreading grin. "I'm just pullin' your leg," he said with a laugh. "You're not the only one who can spin one, Billy."

"Your grandfather never cut down a Christmas tree?"

Travis shook his head, still grinning. "My grandfather would tell everyone we were going to pick a perfect tree, but he'd take me fishing instead and we'd just buy some random tree from a lot on the way home."

Billy dropped the tree into the dirt and pushed Travis's shoulder, which of course led to them trying to put each other in a headlock, which was only made more difficult because they were both laughin' so hard. I looked at Texas, Trav's horse. Even he didn't look impressed. He just twitched his ears and swished his tail in a yep-they're-idiots kind of way. "I know," I told him. "You have no idea what I have to put up with."

"Who are you talking to, Charlie?" Travis asked. They'd apparently stopped wrestling and were lookin' at me.

"Your horse," I answered seriously. "He thinks you're both dickheads."

Travis brushed himself down, though why, I'll never know. Red dust got into everything here; there weren't no escapin' it. "I'll never get used to the Australian display of affection of calling the people you're supposed to like horrible names."

I snorted out a laugh. "You'd think after a year you'd be used to it."

Billy picked up his shovel and offered it to Trav. "Wanna shovel shit?"

"Um, gee, thanks, but no," Trav replied, with an I-ain't-stupid look on his face. "I have a Christmas tree to put up. Considering Christmas is three days away and no one seems to give a shit."

I lifted up the horseshit covered shovel. "Texas does. Bags of it."

He rolled his eyes at me and wiped the sweat from his brow with the back of his hand. "Tell me, how damn hot is it? You know, Christmas should be cold, not one hundred and thirty freakin' degrees." Without waitin' for an answer, he reached behind his head and pulled his T-shirt off. It was one of my old shirts, kinda threadbare, but I didn't mind him wearin' it. It clung to his body when he got all sweaty... Nah, I didn't mind him wearin' it at all. I minded even less when he took it off. Wearing just his jeans, boots and hat, he wrapped the shirt around the tree and lifted it easily onto one shoulder. I watched as the muscles in his back and arms flexed, all shiny with sweat, the way the red dirt smeared on his skin, and a lucky drop of sweat as it ran from the back of his hair, right down his spine and disappeared where his jeans slung low on his arse.

Jesus.

Billy snapped his fingers in my face. "You in there, boss?"

Travis turned around and, realising I'd been busted totally checkin' him out, he grinned. And seeing that Billy wasn't lookin' at him, Travis licked his lips all suggestive like, and ran his free hand over his abs as he turned to walk out.

I flung horseshit at him.

He didn't even turn around. He just laughed. As he walked away, he asked, "I can put this in the living room, right?"

"Would it matter what I said?" I called out after him.

His reply was distant as he reached the house. "Nope."

Billy laughed, and I grumbled as we went back to shovelling shit. When we'd heard the screen door shut, Billy looked up to make sure Travis was gone. "He got no idea what you plannin', does he, boss?"

I smiled as I kept on shovelin'. "None."

I FOUND Travis in the lounge room. He was still shirtless, holding Nugget, and they were staring at the tree. Trav had stuck the tree in an old five-gallon oil drum filled with red dirt and it was shoved in the corner.

"I moved Nugget's bed box," he said. "He's not happy about it." He handed me the said-disgruntled wombat, who snuffled and blinked his disapproval. Travis was still frowning at the tree. "Have you got some tinsel or something?"

"I'm sure we do somewhere." I put Nugget back down on the floor and went in search of Christmas decorations. Truth be told, we hadn't used 'em in years. I got to the hallway and stopped, not sure where to start looking. "Um…"

"Check the linen cupboard," Ma called out from the kitchen.

"Thanks!" Of course that's where they were. Behind the spare blankets on the top shelf was an old plastic tub filled with tinsel and ornaments. I pulled it out and blew the dust off as I walked back into the lounge room.

"Good Lord," Travis mumbled. "When was the last time these were used?"

I shrugged and put the box on the floor. "Dunno. Years, probably. I told ya, we don't really do much in the way of Christmas decorations, Trav."

"You don't do much in the way of Christmas-anything," he mumbled. He reached into the box and pulled out the tinsel. It kind of fell apart in his hand. "Jesus. How old are these?"

I shrugged. "Dunno exactly. Probably as old as me." I rummaged through the box and found some Christmas art I'd done as a kid. It was some Paddle Pop sticks glued into a square with red and green cellophane paper stuck to it with a pipe cleaner looped so it would hang on the tree. I handed it to Travis and rummaged some more. Next thing I pulled out was a glass bauble thing that was faded and all the glitter had long ago fallen off, but you could still read my name.

Travis took it from me. "Oh, Charlie," he said softly. "Is this from when you were a baby?"

"I think so. It's been here forever."

"It has to go on the tree," he said, putting it right on the middle branch. "What else you got in that box?"

I pulled out a knotted string of ball-things. "I think these are older than me."

Trav cringed. "You know, it's too late to order Christmas decorations online and hope to have them delivered before February, but I promise you Charlie, after Christmas, I'm ordering a shit-ton of stuff for next year."

I'd never get tired of hearin' him talk of our future together. "Fair enough."

"Do you really not do anything for Christmas?" he asked. Then he looked at the box of dust-covered ornaments. "Never mind. I can't believe you don't even do gifts."

"Well, we just never really saw a reason for it," I admitted quietly. I was starting to feel guilty about it. "I mean, things are different here now, since you got here. It's more like a family than it ever was, and there were a lot of years even when my dad was alive we still never really did anything. It was just another day."

Travis was frowning. "I know. I'm sorry," he murmured. "I didn't mean anything by it. It's just that Christmas is such a big deal in my parents' house." He tried to smile. "I don't care about gifts or anything like that, but I just thought a tree would be nice."

"The tree's great." And it was. "And who knows, maybe we can start doin' it every year. Or something."

"Like a new tradition?"

"Sure! I mean, it's like I told ya before. We still have a breakfast, then do morning chores, but we usually have the afternoon and evenin' off." I shrugged. "It's different here to what you're used to, I guess."

"I get that, I do," he said gently. He rubbed his hand on

my back. "Can I see what I can make out of these?" he motioned toward the box of decorations.

"Go for it."

Just then Nugget put his two front paws on the oil tin that was holding the tree, reached his little nose up as high as he could and sniffed it. Then he tried to climb up to sniff a little better. "Oh no you don't," Trav said, grabbing Nugget. He shoved him into my arms. "Take him before he trashes everything."

I walked to the door with the fussin' wombat, then turned back to face Travis. "And Trav?"

"Yeah?"

I looked over his naked torso and licked my lips. "I really do like my presents unwrapped."

KNOWING MA WOULD BE YELLIN' for dinner any time soon, I headed back to the house. It was stinkin' hot, my throat was dry and full of dust, my face felt baked by the sun. To be honest, I'd forgotten all about Travis tryin' to Christmasfy the house. But I kicked the dust outta my boots on the front veranda steps, dusted off my jeans, opened the screen door, and stopped.

There, stuck to the front door, was a homemade Christmas wreath. Now, it was the most Australian lookin' Christmas decoration I think I'd ever seen. It was a wire coat hanger bent all outta shape into a sort-of circle, and wrapped around it was some of those red baubles-on-a-string, silver tinsel, and a bunch of twigs of eucalyptus and peppercorn from the trees out the back.

It made me smile just lookin' at it.

"You like it?"

I didn't realise Trav had seen me lookin' at his handi-work. "It's great. Very Australian."

"Funny that," he said with a laugh. "Just so happens the only trees I had to get leaves from are Australian."

I leaned in closer to the wreath and breathed in deep. It's funny how the smell of something can run a memory through your mind like it was yesterday. "It smells like summer when I was a kid, climbin' those trees and playin' for hours."

Travis grinned at me, the kind of grin that told me I'd just said somethin' completely right. "Thank you."

CHAPTER TWO

MISTLETOES AND A BROKEN NOSE

"WHAT ELSE DID YOU DO?" I asked, lookin' in the hallway. I couldn't see anything else particularly Christmassy. But Trav was out of his jeans and wearing shorts and a t-shirt, bein' all barefoot, like he was done for the day. "You put on a shirt, I can see that much."

He snorted. "Well, it's too hot for jeans and boots. And you might like me shirtless, but I don't think Ma did."

"She's such a spoilsport."

"I heard that," Ma hollered from the kitchen.

Travis chuckled and nodded toward the lounge room. "I finished the tree," he said and disappeared through the open doorway. I followed him to find the pine tree he'd brought in earlier now covered in tinsel, ornaments, and baubles. "I know you think the whole Christmas thing is kinda silly, but—"

"I love it," I said. "The tree. I mean, I love what you've done to it."

"I didn't have much to work with," he said. The corner of his mouth pulled down in a frown. "And it was all pretty old. I hung up all the things you made as a kid. I just wanted to do something." He shrugged again. "I mean, it's Christmas."

"Trav."

"And I know you guys aren't big on the whole festive thing out here," he said. "But I just thought it'd be nice, ya know? It's Gracie's first Christmas. Granted, she's only four weeks old but that's not the point."

"Trav."

"It's about building memories, Charlie," he said softly. "Family memories. Not just with everyone here, but *our* family. Ours start now. This is *our* first real Christmas too and I just thought it might be nice if you, you know, thought it was special too."

I stepped in close to him and softly pressed my lips to his. "I do. And I gotta say, Trav, when you talk family as in me and you, it does somethin' to me in here," I said, putting his hand to my chest. "Can you feel that? Makes my heart go beat itself all outta rhythm."

He shook his head at me. "Why do you have to go saying stuff like that?" he whispered, before he nudged his nose to mine. "Being all sweet and shit."

"Same reason you do your nose nudgin' thing," I whispered back, givin' him an almost-kiss. "But I don't need it to be Christmas Day to remind me how lucky I am. I wake up every day with you in my bed, so I *know* how lucky I am."

He put his hand to my face and kissed me harder. It was a deep kiss, an I-love-you kind of kiss, and just when I was imagining takin' him into our bedroom....

He headbutted my nose.

"Ow!" he cried, taking a step back. I might have seen that he was holdin' his foot if I weren't looking through tears.

"What the fuck, Trav?!" I said, holding the bridge of my

nose, tryin' to ignore the blinding spear of pain that was shootin' through my skull. My eyes were waterin' and my nose... shit, my nose.

"Nugget bit me!"

By this time, Ma was standin' in the doorway. "What on earth happened?"

"Nugget bit me," he said again, still holding his foot. I could see now there was blood on his foot, seepin' through his fingers.

"I think you broke my nose," I told him, still holding the bridge of my nose. I could taste blood in the back of my throat. There weren't any blood dripping out, but it sure felt broke to me.

"Come into the kitchen, both of you," Ma said.

I followed her in, holding my nose with my head back, and Trav limped in behind us. Nugget, the little shit, was nowhere to be found. I pulled out a chair for him and me, and when we sat down, I pulled his injured foot up onto my thigh. The blood was still pourin' freely from two very distinct puncture wounds.

"That freakin' wombat hates me," he said.

"No he doesn't," I was quick to tell him. "He just doesn't like anyone getting too close to me."

Ma handed me a bag of frozen peas for my nose and put a wet cloth on Trav's foot. "Well, he got you pretty good," Ma said. "Maybe he bit so hard 'cause he's used to biting you when you're wearing boots."

"Oh no," Travis shook his head. "He knew exactly what he was doing."

"Does it need stitches?" I asked.

"Mm," Ma looked closer. "Don't think so."

I took the bag of frozen peas from my face and looked at his foot. The bite was just down from his two smallest toes.

At least the blood had stopped a bit, but the bite itself looked deep. "Did he get the bone? 'Cause that'll be a trip to the doctors if he did. It'll get infected for sure."

"Great," Travis grumbled. "I'll get mad-wombat disease."

I laughed, which reminded me with another stab of pain that my nose was broken. "Ugh," I said, putting the bag of peas back onto my face.

"I'm sorry I headbutted you," Trav said. "I didn't mean to. I wasn't expecting the evil wombat to sink his fangs into me."

"'S'okay," I said, sounding all nasally. "I'm sorry he bit you."

"I've been trying to keep him away from that tree for the last hour," Travis said. He winced as Ma dabbed the cloth to his foot. "How's your nose?"

I put the peas on the table and let him have a look. "Am I still beautiful?"

Travis barked out a laugh. "Oh yeah."

Ma looked up from bathing Trav's foot and gave my face the once over. "It's not broken."

It's possible I pouted. "Feels like it."

Ma poured some Dettol into a bowl with warm water. Travis scrunched up his nose. "What's that stuff?"

"Disinfectant," Ma said.

"The smell of my childhood," I said with a smile, which of course made my entire skull hurt.

Ma lifted my hand, holding the peas back to my face. "Keep the peas on it or you'll have two black eyes."

Travis frowned again. "I'm really sorry."

"Don't feel bad," I told him from behind the peas. "I've had worse. Hey Ma, remember that time when I was a kid and I got bucked off that bull and face-planted into the railing. Now *that* was a broken nose."

Ma grumbled at me. "Do I ever. Your face was so swollen you looked like you fell face first into a drum of hornets."

I lifted the peas off again. "That was fun."

Travis raised one eyebrow. "Fun?"

"Not the face-planting. The bull riding."

Ma gave me her best glare. "Don't you even think about bull riding again, you hear me?"

"I wouldn't," I said, but I think my smile made it look like I was lyin'.

Ma held my face and inspected my nose, gently feeling along the bridge with her fingers. Then without warning or without sayin' a damn thing, she held the back of my head in one hand, took my nose between her two fingers and yanked it upwards.

"Ow!" I yelled. "Ma!"

Then she whacked the peas back on my face with the finesse and gentleness of an unbroken brumby. "Quit your whinging, Charlie. You've had worse."

All Travis could do was laugh.

"I thought you said it wasn't broken?" I asked from behind the frozen peas. I was grateful they couldn't see my eyes watering.

"Now it's not," she answered.

"Jesus H. Christ," I mumbled. Then Ma proceeded to put some soft gauze on Travis's foot and strapped it like he was made of glass. "How come he gets the special treatment?" Okay, so now it was possible I was sulking.

"I needed to do it quickly," Ma replied.

Just then, George walked into the kitchen and stopped when he saw us. "Did I miss the tickets to the circus?"

"Oh har har," I said, pulling the peas off my face to show him my nose.

"Hmm," he pursed his lips as he inspected my face. "You've had worse."

"Is there a sign out front sayin' 'Leave your sympathy at the door'?"

"Dunno," George answered in that dry drawl of his. "I came in through the back."

Travis and Ma laughed. I put the peas back on my face and ignored them all.

CHAPTER THREE

OH COME, ALL YE FAITHFUL

SURPRISINGLY, I didn't have two black eyes. I didn't even have one. Maybe just a bit of discolouration in the corners of my eyes, but there was an angry red line across the bridge of my nose. "Maybe it'll bruise up by the morning," I said, getting into bed.

Trav was already lyin' down with just the sheet over him—it was too hot for anything else—and his bandaged foot sticking out the side. "How's the foot-biter?"

"Well, he still weren't too keen on comin' out from behind the lounge, but he's in bed now, all snuggled up with Rumble Bear. He said he was sorry for bitin' ya."

"Did he now?"

"Yep. Said he prefers the leather of your boot, for what it's worth."

Trav shook his head at me and his smilin' faded to frownin' when he looked at my nose. "Looks sore," he said. "And I am really sorry."

"You gonna make it up to me?" I asked. "Because I'm pretty sure I read somewhere that blowjobs are good for broken noses."

Travis snorted. "Oh, really? And where did you read that?"

"In the 'What to do when you break your boyfriend's nose' handbook."

He grinned. "Was there a chapter on feet-biting wombats?"

"Nope. All about the boyfriend. Mostly just dick-suckin' and making him cups of tea."

His blue eyes shone as he laughed. "Is that so?"

"Yeah. And Trav?"

"Yeah?"

"I don't want a cup of tea."

"No?"

"Well, maybe with breakfast, but not right now."

"Right now you want the dick-sucking?"

I nodded. "It was conditional though."

"I'm sure it was."

"It had to be reciprocated. I'm sure there was a clause in there somewhere about if my face is too sore because of well, you know, the broken nose, then I should consider letting him... you know, do something else...."

Trav smirked. "Such as?"

I could feel myself blush. "You gonna make me say it?"

He nodded. "I've told you before you don't have to be embarrassed about telling me what you want."

I cringed. "Well, you didn't break my arse, so I was thinkin'..."

"Yeah?"

"You could, you know, have me that way instead."

His smile was slow and salacious. "You want me to fuck you, Charlie?" he whispered.

I swallowed hard, but managed to nod.

Trav pulled himself up against the headboard and

propped a pillow behind his head. Then he patted his chest. "Straddle me," he said. There weren't no politeness to it, it was more a demand.

I was quick to comply. I was only wearing briefs and he pulled them down at the front and took my already-gettin' hard dick out. He licked his lips and looked up at me. "Hold on to the headboard, Charlie," he said gruffly, then he licked the head of my cock.

I gripped the wooden bedhead as he took me into his mouth. He put his hands on my hips and guided me, in and out, sucking me so hard. *God, it feels good.* He took me deep and slow, then sucked on the head, workin' me for what felt like hours of heaven, yet nowhere near long enough. And then he did that thing with his tongue...

"Trav..." I tried to warn him.

He replied with a moan and dug his fingers into my hips before exploring just that little bit further. He was reachin' around so he could tease my arse and balls before takin' me all the way.

And I was done. That feelin' of pure pleasure, wound tight in my balls, lurched, and my orgasm barrelled through me. Travis moaned as he drank me down and my whole body buzzed from the aftershocks.

I all but fell to the side of him. My muscles were spent from hangin' onto the headboard so tight, and I didn't even feel Trav move until he pulled me around like I weighed next to nothing. I was flat on my stomach—still all heavy and boneless—my briefs were still pulled down, and he was pourin' lube over my arse. All I could do was moan and raise my hips for his fingers to stretch me.

I loved this. I loved giving myself to him like this. He could do with me what he wanted, and I would let him. I was his. He owned me, in every sense of the word. And after a time, when I was all but beggin' him, he put his cock to my hole and pushed inside me. Slow and deep, he took his time, and took me to that place— that place of bliss and stars—where only he could take me.

His legs were on the outside of mine, one of his arms wound under my chest, and he lifted my head back so he could kiss my neck and whisper dirty things in my ear.

Oh, how he knew I loved his dirty mouth.

"This is what you wanted," he breathed. His lips were hot on my ear, his cock was deep in my arse. "You love it when I fuck you like this."

I whined. He knew damn well I did....

"I love being inside you," he moaned. He leaned back a bit, pushing deeper inside me still, and ran his hands down my arms. He threaded his fingers with mine above our heads and rocked his hips. I lifted my arse so he could thrust a little harder. "Jesus Charlie, I'm gonna come."

"Please." I don't think I meant to say it out loud.

His grip on me tightened and he thrust harder and harder, deeper and deeper until he cried out and stilled. I could feel him pulse inside me as he came, and finally he collapsed on top of me.

"Fuck."

I chuckled. "Yep."

He kissed my shoulder with smiling lips, but never moved to get off me. After a while, he asked, "How's your nose?"

In that moment, I could feel nothing but spongy bones and a pleasant ache in my arse. "What nose?"

He snorted and rolled to the side, taking me with him. He tightened his arm around me, and I immediately wanted him back inside me. The longer I lay there, the more I wanted it. I wiggled my arse back onto his softening cock. He sounded sleepy. "Again?"

"Are you Santa Claus?"

He chuckled into my shoulder blade. "You mean, do I come only once?"

I smiled and ground my arse onto his dick. He slid into me easier the second time, and I can truly vouch, that Travis Craig ain't nothing like Santa.

CHAPTER FOUR

ALL TRAV WANTS FOR CHRISTMAS IS… HEATSTROKE?

THE NEXT DAY, the day before Christmas Eve, Trav was to head out with Billy into the Western paddock, checkin' cattle, fences, and water troughs. They left long before sunup to beat the heat of the day, and it gave me plenty of time to make last-minute emails and phone calls to make sure everything was going to plan.

It was weird to be excited about Christmas.

Part of me wished real hard that it wasn't a surprise. I wanted to share this part with Travis. This excitement, the build-up. But part of me couldn't wait to see his face on Christmas morning.

So I set about gettin' some office work done until Ma called us for lunch. Travis and Billy weren't back yet—that weren't too surprising—and they radioed in to say they were two hours away. So we kept some lunch aside for them and kept on about our day. The general rule of the Outback summer was to work early and late, taking the hottest few hours of the day off. Usually stayin' indoors outta the sun was the best way to spend it, though I normally found myself in the office getting paperwork done.

I smiled to myself when I heard the old Cruiser come into the yard. It was always a relief to know when people were back, but knowin' Trav was somewhere close was a comfort I couldn't explain.

The screen door banged and there was a sound of boots on the floorboards. Ma responded with, "Lunch is on the table."

Though I was a little disappointed Trav didn't stick his head around the door, I heard the quiet murmur of voices and the clanging of cutlery in the dining room, and figurin' they'd be starving hungry, I didn't want to bother them while they ate. But when they were done, it wasn't Travis who came to see me. It was Billy.

"Hey, boss," he said, looking a little unsure. "He didn't want me to say nothin', but Mr Travis ain't feelin' too good."

I got to my feet. "Where is he?"

"Don't think he's moved from the dining table, boss."

That was exactly where I found him. He had his head in his hands, his plate of half-eaten lunch still in front of him. He looked up at me and I could see then he weren't his usual colour. He frowned. "Billy told ya, didn't he?"

"Yes, thankfully," I said walking over to him. "Trav, you look like shit."

"Gee, thanks."

I put my hand on his shoulder and he was hot to the touch. *Too* hot. I put my hand on his chest, then on his forehead and on the top of his head. He was cooked. "Ma!"

It must have been my tone, because not a moment later, Ma appeared in the doorway. "What's wrong?"

Just then, Trav's head kind of lolled back and he almost fell of the chair before I grabbed him. "I think Trav's heat-struck."

"Get him into the bathroom," Ma said, quickly dashing off.

I pulled Trav to his feet and half-led, half-carried him into our bathroom. I leaned him against the counter and pulled off his boots and socks, then ripped his shirt over his head. "What were you doin' out there?"

"The fourth bore," he said weakly. "It weren't running like it should, so I greased the piston and recalibrated it."

"You were in the bore house?"

He nodded.

"Jesus, Travis. How long were you in there for?"

He shrugged. "Twenty, maybe thirty minutes."

"It must be over fifty degrees in that bore house, Trav!" I ran his shirt under the tap, soaking it through, and wiped it over his face, neck, and chest. "It's a corrugated iron oven in summer! You damn near cooked yourself."

"It wasn't too bad when I was in there," he said quietly. "I mean, it was hot."

"That's the thing with heatstroke, Trav. It creeps up on ya afterwards and knocks you for six later."

Ma was beside me then, with a bag of ice cubes wrapped in a tea-towel. She handed it to me and took the wet shirt. "Alternate putting that behind his neck and on his chest and on top of his head," she said. "We need to get his core temperature down."

Ma put the shirt in the sink again and rinsed the dust out of it before putting it back on his arms and shoulders.

That was when she noticed a hickey on his collarbone. She inspected it closer, then turned and swatted me on the arm. "Oh, I thought that was an allergic welt or a spider bite or something."

Trav snorted weakly. "At least we know where Nugget gets his biting from." Then he shucked the icepack off the back of his neck and looked a paler shade of green. "Feel like I'm gonna be sick."

He made it to the toilet just in time, and when he was done, he looked even paler than before. Ma put a strip thermometer over his forehead and we watched the numbers climb from green 37 to a frightening red 40. "Yep, heatstroke," Ma said. "Rub the ice bag all over his chest and on the top of his head," she told me, then she started inspecting the back of his neck and into his hair.

"Travis, do you remember seeing any redback spiders?"

Trav shook his head. "No."

Ma nodded. "Charlie, get him into the shower. Check him over for any kind of bites, just in case, then put him to bed." And with that, she was gone, the bathroom door pulled closed behind her.

I undid his jeans and pulled them down his thighs. It was always a pretty clear indication on Travis's well-bein' when there were no sex jokes, especially when I was kneelin' in front of him trying to get his jeans off. I ran the shower with the cold only, which was lukewarm at best. The thing about livin' in the desert and livin' off rainwater was that the rain-tanks sat on the baking ground like everything else.

"Remind me when you're feelin' better about looking into puttin' tanks underground," I mumbled, helping him into the already-too-small shower.

"Huh?" He looked confused.

"Later," I told him. "Just put your head under the water. Do you feel sore or itchy anywhere?"

He took a second to answer. "Nope. I didn't get bitten by anything, Charlie. I just feel sick. And hot. Really hot."

"You have heatstroke, Trav," I reminded him. "It can cook your brain if you're not careful."

He leaned forward and rested his forehead on his arms on the shower wall, and I stood outside the shower but quickly ran the soap over his back and shoulders. I figured cleanin' off the dust before he got into bed would be a good idea. The red dust swirled around his feet and I scrubbed down his legs as well.

"Well, I ain't near dead enough to know that I like your hands on me in the shower," he mumbled.

I snorted out a laugh. "You must be feeling a bit better." Then I asked, "How much water have you drank today?"

He seemed to think for a while. "Dunno. A bit. Two water bottles, I think."

"Open your mouth, drink the water," I instructed. "Small mouthfuls."

He did that for a while and then I shut the water off and towelled him down before tying it around his waist. "Come on, into bed."

"I feel a bit better."

"Don't argue with me on this, Trav. Into bed. Please."

He hardly argued. With no more than a miserable pout, he took himself, slow and steady, to our room and sat on the bed. I switched on the ceiling fan and made him lie down, and Ma came in with a pedestal fan and the bag of ice, and when he was sufficiently fussed over, he closed his eyes and dozed. I sat beside him, movin' the ice pack around and wipin' him down with a wet cloth.

There weren't nothin' worse than watching the person you love bein' so sick.

"Remember when I busted my knee?" he asked. His eyes were still closed. "You sat there like that."

"I thought you were asleep."

"Just resting."

"You need to stop making a habit of me needing to sit here watching you all helpless in bed."

He smiled, though his eyes stayed shut. "You love me all helpless in bed."

"You know what I mean."

"I do." He let out a slow and steady breath. "Sorry. I just thought it wouldn't take me long to fix the pump, and I didn't realise how hot it was in there. I should know better. Sorry."

I took his hand and gave it a squeeze. "It's okay, Trav. I'm just glad you're okay."

Then I remembered his surprise Christmas present.

I almost told him. Right then and there, I almost told him what I'd done. The words were on the tip of my tongue....

"Might just sleep a little," he mumbled.

"Good idea," I whispered, and bringin' his hand to my mouth, I kissed his knuckles. "I'll stay right here."

He gave me a smilin'-sigh, and not a moment later, a soft snore. And I watched him. I told myself I was monitoring his breathing, being careful to keep him as cool as possible, which in forty-degree summer heat weren't strictly the easiest thing. But truthfully, I just liked to watch him sleep. Not in some creepy way. More like in an I-still-can't-believe-it kinda way. It amazed me still that this man was mine. And I had no doubt, I'd still be amazed forty years from now.

I lightly dragged the cold wet cloth across his chest and over his forehead. He stirred a little, mumblin' somethin' I couldn't quite make out, before bein' all peaceful again. And he'd never looked so handsome. This is what *in sickness and in health* meant. That I would sit by his bedside after he damn near cooked his foolish self in an iron shed.

There was a soft knock at the door, and after a long second, Ma poked her head in. "How is he?" she whispered.

"Asleep."

She nodded, and seeing he was covered up with the towel around his waist, she came into the room. She gently laid the strip thermometer over his forehead, and this time it read a much better thirty-nine degrees. "He's getting better," she said, relieved. "Keep doing what you're doing," she whispered. She handed me the thermometer. "Check him every thirty minutes. If his temperature stops coming down, we'll need to call the doctor."

"Thanks." I nodded and looked at the black strip of thermometer in my hand. It was about one inch wide, eight inches long, made from x-ray film type stuff, and had numbers up the side of it. Ma had used it forever and swore by it, but I had to wonder how else I could use it...

Ma raised one eyebrow at me. "It goes on his forehead, Charlie. His *forehead*."

"I know!"

She hummed. "I swear sometimes I can read your mind."

Travis chuckled, makin' me and Ma look at him. "Thought you were asleep," I said.

"Trying to," he mumbled. "It goes on my forehead Charlie..."

Ma nodded. "See?"

"While Ma's in the room anyway," Trav added sleepily. His eyes were barely open.

Ma sighed and snatched the thermometer back off me. "And Billy was worried. I'll tell him you'll be just fine." She walked to the door but before she got there, she said, "Dinner will be in two hours. You," she said, lookin' pointedly at me, "will be at the table. And you, Travis Craig, can eat in here." Then as she walked down the hallway, she finished with, "No funny business, ya hear?"

I fell back into the chair beside the bed with a sigh. "You just got full-named."

Trav was almost back to sleep, but he murmured, "Reminds me of being at home." I don't know whether it was bein' heat-sick or homesick, but he frowned.

I leaned over and kissed his still-too-hot forehead. "Go back to sleep," I whispered to him. I set about keeping him cool with the icepack and wet cloth, wishin' it was Christmas already.

CHAPTER FIVE

'TWAS THE DAY BEFORE CHRISTMAS

LIKE ANY OTHER DAY, I was up before the sun. When the dogs and horses were fed and watered and as breakfast was near ready, I went in to check on Trav. He was all stretched out onto my side, his long legs and arms takin' up the whole bed. The sheet was barely coverin' the swell of his arse. His well-defined shoulders and back made me wanna crawl in there beside him and never leave.

I put my hand on his head. He felt a more normal temperature. "Hey, sleepyhead."

"Mmm." He stirred, then startled awake and sat up. "Shit. What time is it?"

"It's stayin'-in-bed time for you. You need to take the day off."

"What for?"

"Trav, you were quite sick yesterday."

"I feel fine." It was only then that he seemed to take stock of how he actually felt. He shook his head. "I'm just tired."

"A day of rest for you. Doctor's orders. Well, Ma's orders, but around here it's the same thing."

He fell back on the bed and put his hand to his forehead. "How can I still be tired? I've slept so much."

I put my hand to his chest. "Your body temperature feels back to normal, but your energy levels are depleted. Trav, you almost lost consciousness yesterday; your brain almost cooked in your skull. You need a day of rest. Lots of water and lyin' around."

He sighed. "Will you be close by?"

"Yep. In and out of the homestead all day. I'm tellin' everyone to take it easy today. We'll do just what needs doin' and that'll be about it, I reckon. You know, bein' Christmas Eve and all."

Trav scoffed and rolled his eyes. "Thought you said no one cared about Christmas out here."

"We don't. Not really. I just don't want anyone keelin' over on me."

"God forbid. For a minute there I considered revoking your Scrooge status. I thought you might have found some Christmas spirit."

"Nah. I'm still Charlie 'Scrooge' Sutton. The last thing I want is Work Safe out here reaming me for workin' ya's too hard in the heat."

He snorted out a laugh. "Yes, because really, if anyone's gonna be reaming you, it better be me."

I tweaked his nipple, making him squirm. "Damn straight it better be you."

Trav licked his lips and put his hand on my thigh, slowly creepin' his fingers up to my groin. "I'm sure I'm feeling good enough to—"

"Charlie!" Ma called out.

Trav let his hand fall away and gave out a for-fuck's-sake sigh. "How does she know? Every time we—"

"Breakfast!"

I laughed and stood up from the edge of the bed. "I'll bring you something first."

He groaned as I walked out and was still grumbling when I came back in with a tray of a full breakfast, juice, coffee, and water. I knew Travis, and if I were expecting him to sleep the day away, the second best way to get him snoozin' was food. Sex was the first option, but seein's that was out of the question with everyone in and around the house all day, a belly full of food was the only way to keep him down.

And an hour later when I went back in to get the tray, he'd eaten everything and was sound asleep. His foot—Band-Aids now covered where Nugget had bitten him—was sticking out of the bed and the thin cotton sheet draped over his thighs, but the rest of him was on full glorious view. I swear he slept naked to tease me.

Trav was the most hyperactive guy I'd ever known, and keepin' him well-rested weren't strictly easy. When I came in from the shed at mornin' tea time, he was showered and lazin' on the lounge, lecturing Nugget about the Christmas tree. He held up the wombat so Nugget was facing me. "He keeps trying to kill the tree, Charlie."

I looked at the offending wombat. Nugget twitched his nose, then seemed to grin at me which of course made me laugh.

Travis groaned as he stood up and shoved him in my arms. "Here. You look after him. He won't listen to anyone but you anyway."

I heard Travis close the bathroom door and, with Nugget burrowin' under my arm, made my way into the kitchen to where Ma and Nara were flat out busy. The centre table was covered in eggs, fruit, proving dough, and flour. "Can I do anything to help?" I asked.

Ma looked at the doorway, clearly checking to see if Travis was close by. "Everything going well?"

I whispered my reply. "Operation Christmas Present is a go. Got an email this morning sayin' everything's going exactly to plan."

Ma smiled but looked back at the door. "I know Travis needs to rest, but he's going stir crazy. He can't stay inside doing nothing. He's been in here two dozen times wanting to know what we're cooking different things for, Charlie. He's gonna catch on that we're up to something."

"I'll find something for him to do in the office. That'll keep him out of your way," I said softly. "But first it's cuppa time for me and snack time for this little guy." I dug Nugget out of my armpit and held him like a footy instead so he could see what Ma and Nara were doing.

Ma shook her head at us. "Look at you two. Never thought I'd see the day."

"If he keeps drivin' Trav up the wall, you won't be seein' him no more."

"Won't be seeing who no more? Me or the evil wombat?" Travis asked from the doorway.

I laughed. "Who do you think?"

He grumbled as he walked in and scratched Nugget's head. "Sometimes I wonder."

I bumped my hip to his. "You know that ain't true." He barely smiled.

Ma put a cup of tea on the table and Nara cut up enough apple and carrot for Nugget, so I sat down and pulled out a chair for Trav as well. I took sips of tea in between holding and feeding Nugget chunks of carrot, and me and Trav shared the apple, but Ma was right. Travis was miserable. And bored. And a bored Travis was never a good thing. "Hey, I was thinking now might be a good time to show you how to do the books."

Travis looked at me with disbelief. "Yeah, right."

"No, I'm serious. You should know how to do it all in case I can't, for whatever reason." I shrugged. "And you need to stay out of the heat and you're bored outta your mind, so yeah, now's the perfect time."

"What do you mean by doing the books exactly?" he asked.

"Accounts, ordering, debtors, creditors, stocktaking, that kind of thing."

Travis blinked, but I could see the excitement in his eyes. "Really?"

"Absolutely."

He finally grinned. "Okay, cool." He gave Nugget another scratch on the forehead. "I don't know how he can be so cute and so infuriating at the same time."

"He takes after me," I said. Nugget looked up at me and snuffled his agreement. "Come on, to bed with you, little guy. We've got work to do." I stole some more of Nara's cut apples and put Nugget and the fruit in his bed box, where he couldn't trash Trav's Christmas tree, and I took Trav into the office.

I switched on the fan. "You not too hot in here?"

Trav shook his head. "No, I'm fine."

"How much water have you had to drink today?" I asked.

"Oh, don't you start," he mumbled. "Ma's been shoving a bottle of water down my throat every hour on the hour, so I'm really, more than fine."

I snorted. "Just checking."

I opened up my laptop without thinking how my emails

showed up on screen. The word "confirmation" flashed up, and I quickly exited out before Trav saw anything. The last thing I needed was for him to read something about his present arriving tomorrow and spoiling everything. Especially since the whole thing had been planned for weeks. It'd be a shame to ruin it the day before Christmas.

"So," I started. "You click on this...." And so for the next two hours, I showed him how, where, and when I entered in data. It was a specific accounts program that we'd customised to suit our business so it was really simple, and Travis picked it up in no time. He was cross-referencing dates, invoices to receipts, product codes and numbers and figures like a pro, asking a question here and there, but otherwise doing it all by himself. I, on the other hand, sat there with my legs stretched out onto the desk reading the latest copy of Farmer's Annual. Every so often, I'd catch Trav lookin' at my thighs instead of the screen, and I figured the distraction was payback for him sleeping naked this morning.

Ma stuck her head around the door frame. "Kitchen's closed until dinner shift. It's too hot in there. You want something, you can get it yourself."

I gave her a smile. "No worries. Go put your feet up for a few."

She looked pointedly at my feet on my desk. "I plan to. Don't wake me for nothing."

The house was quiet for all of five seconds before Trav stood up and walked to the door. He closed it, locked it, and walked back to stand in front of me. He parked his arse on my desk and slowly undid the fly of his shorts and gave his dick a long stroke. He was almost fully hard already. "I've wanted this since this morning."

I looked up at him. "Um, Trav...?"

He stood up away from the desk, and with his fist around the base of his dick, he put his cockhead to my lips. *Right then.* No need to guess what Travis wanted. So I opened my mouth for him.

He was a whole lotta less grumpy after that.

CHAPTER SIX

IT'S AN AUSTRALIAN OUTBACK KIND OF TINSEL

"NO NEED TO LOOK SO SMUG," I said, looking up at Trav.

Wearing his post-orgasm smirk and half-lidded eyes, he was now leaning his arse against my desk in front of me from where I still sat in the chair. "True. You should be the smug one," he drawled. Then he put his fingers under my chin and whispered, "You're very good at giving head." He leaned down and kissed me, tasting himself. "Swap me places. It's your turn."

I got to my feet and leaned right against him, kissin' him nice and slow. But then I heard a voice followed by the back screen door. I growled in frustration, and maybe a little disappointment, but went and unlocked the office door.

It was Trudy and little baby Gracie. "Oh boy, it's much cooler in here," Trudy said. She looked hot and bothered. Actually she looked exhausted.

"Everything okay?" I asked.

"Sure. Just wondering if there was an old pedestal fan not in use I could borrow. Can't seem to keep this little one cool enough." Little Gracie was so tiny. Well, as tiny as babies are, I supposed, and she was wearing just a nappy, but she looked hot too. "Bacon's looking over the air conditioner in our place. It's just not working like it should. I keep giving her baths and wiping her down with a damp cloth, but it's just *hot*."

"I know just how she feels," Trav said, drawing his thumb down Gracie's cheek. "That was me yesterday."

"Stay in here," I told her. "I'll get the pedestal fan from our room for ya, then I'll go give Bacon a hand. We'll get it fixed twice as fast. But you should stay in here until then."

I didn't really give her a chance to argue. I put the fan in the lounge room and along with the bouncer we kept in the main house, saving Trudy from havin' to bring one with her every time she came up from their place. By the time I put on my boots and hat, Trav had taken charge. He had Gracie in the bouncer under the fan, talking baby-speak to her, and Trudy was standing in the hallway.

"He told me to go get some sleep while I can," Trudy said.

I couldn't help but smile. "He's bossy, isn't he?"

"Well, if I'm under house-arrest, I may as well be helping out when I'm able," Trav said, not taking his eyes off Gracie. He was slowly bouncing her and bein' all big smiles and bright eyes. It was clear that he adored her.

I had to admit, seeing him with her did something to my insides. I had never even contemplated a family of my own, not until he mentioned the other week about getting married and maybe havin' kids together. It was just something I never dreamed possible. But now... well now I had to lot to think about.

Trudy patted my arm and gave me a look-at-you-looking-at-him smile, and I felt myself blush a dozen shades of red. "You should," I said, changing subjects. "Go and have a sleep, that is. While you can. I'll go see what's up with your air conditioner."

As soon as I walked outside, the dry air sucked the breath from my lungs. It was a baking heat, the sun was sweltering and I could feel the heat of the ground through the soles of my boots.

It sure was a hot one.

The red horizon was shimmering like a mirage, and in the hundred metre walk to the staff cottages, I could feel the sweat already running down my back. It made me smile. The blistering heat of the desert was disgusting and gritty, dangerous, and an earthly reminder of just who was in charge out here.

I loved it.

Or maybe I was just smilin' because life was good.

I had to tell myself to stop grinnin' like an idiot when I got to Trudy and Bacon's cottage. Bacon had the casing off the air conditioning motor, which was, thankfully, on the shaded side of the house.

"Trudy's havin' a kip," I told him. "Travis is on baby-sittin' duty, and I'm here to give you a hand."

"Thanks, mate," he replied, handing me a wrench. And as we worked on the motor, just givin' it a service and cleanin' the dust out of everything, I thought about what he called me.

Mate.

It wasn't too long ago he called me boss.

I had to admit, I liked the difference.

After a while of working in silence, when Bacon was cleaning out the filters, he asked, "So, Travis hasn't clued in yet?"

"Nope."

"He's gonna hate you."

I laughed. "No he won't." Then I made a face. "Well, hopefully not for too long. He still thinks we think Christmas is no big deal."

"Well, this is first year it's been different," Bacon said. "For both of us. Been a helluva year, huh?"

We slid the casing back over the motor and started to screw it back down. "It sure has."

"Whoda thought this time last year that I'd be a dad," Bacon said. "Or that you'd..." He paused to find the right words.

Come out? Meet Travis? Ask him to stay? Fall in love? Be happy?

I finished his sentence for him. "Have everything I ever wanted? Certainly not me." I sighed. "It's all so different now."

"It is," he agreed, wiping the sweat from his brow. "And I wouldn't change a thing."

It was then I noticed the garden hoe leaning against the veranda. Each cottage was a two-bedroom house on piers and footings, which meant there was a good two foot clearance under each house. I bet anything you like, if I walked to the back door, there'd be a long-handled shovel or something similar there as well, and having that kinda thing by the door around here could only mean one thing. "You got a snake?"

"Yeah, saw him this morning," Bacon said. "Brown snake, about five foot long."

Shit. "You should have said something."

He shrugged. "Never used to worry too much. But now with Grace... Well, it's different now."

I nodded. "Yeah, it is." I picked up the hoe. "Come on, we'll hunt it out."

Now if anyone else did what I did, I'd be pissed. If

Travis did it, I'd be *royally* pissed and serve him a lecture about bein' three hours from hospital and bein' plain old stupid. But it was me, and I'd done this kinda thing a hundred times before. Now, I was strictly all for the conservation of animals, and this snake was truly only lookin' for somewhere cool to sleep, but it was just like Bacon said: things were different now. Grace lived in this house, and if a newborn baby was ever bitten by a brown snake, you could forget the three hour trip to hospital. She'd probably be dead before they could run her the hundred metres to the homestead.

So, with the longest stick I could find, I crawled on my belly under their house. It didn't take long to find the snake, coiled up in the cool dirt by a house pier. It weren't too happy to see me, nor me it, if I was bein' truthful. Meeting one of the deadliest snakes on the planet, face-to-face, wasn't how I pictured spending Christmas Eve. Pokin' it with a stick earned me a hiss, but I could manoeuvre it to keep its head away from me. Eventually it got the message and backed off, slitherin' out the other side of the house. "He's comin' your way!" I called.

"I see him," Bacon yelled.

I got the hell out from under the house and raced around the back to see Bacon take a swing with the shovel. With perfect aim, he relieved the snake's body of its head. Of course, even headless, it still squirmed and thrashed. Bacon shuddered. "Ugh. I hate how they do that."

"Yeah, it's gross. Good shot by the way."

"Thanks." He let out a bit of a laugh. "Thanks for going under the house for it."

"No worries. Just don't tell Travis. Or Ma."

He laughed. "Deal."

I picked up the tail of the snake and nodded toward the detached head. "You good with that?"

"Yeah, I'll go bury it." He looked at the long, still-wriggling body of the snake. "What you gonna do with that?"

I shrugged. "Tell Travis we'll bake it up like some Aussie Christmas delicacy or some shit."

He barked out a laugh.

And then like some Christmas miracle, the wind changed direction. "Feel that?" I asked.

Bacon grinned. "Yeah. Means cool change."

I could feel the sweat on my skin coolin' in the breeze already. "Halle-freakin-lujah." I nodded back to his house. "Go inside, enjoy your air conditioning. I'll tell Trudy it's all good when she wakes up."

I left him to it and walked back up to the house, feeling the already-cooler breeze on my back. I found Travis on the back veranda with little Gracie enjoying the cool change. "How nice is that breeze?" he asked, then did a double take at what I was holding. "Charlie, what the hell is that?"

I slung the snake over a low-lyin' branch of the tree in the backyard. "Outback Christmas tinsel."

Travis stared at me. "Um, I don't think tinsel should bleed. Or be headless. Just saying."

I climbed the veranda steps and gave Trav a quick kiss. "It was under Gracie's house, and that just won't do." I kissed the little girl on the forehead. "That just won't do at all."

"Did you get the air conditioning working again?"

"Yep. Just needed a clean out. Is Trudy awake?"

"Nope. Ma's in the kitchen and threatened bodily harm to anyone who wakes a new mother."

"Fair enough."

Trav looked back at the snake. "You just gonna leave that there?"

"Yep. It'll wriggle till the sun goes down," I told him. "Bacon buried the head. The venom can still kill ya, even when the damn thing is cut in two."

Just then, Billy came out of the shed and up toward the house. He saw the snake. "Oh, thanks boss. Fresh dinner!"

Trav's nostrils flared, and his mouth formed a watery line. "Serious?"

"Makes real good eating," Billy said, inspecting the snake.

Trav looked at me. "Is he serious?"

I shrugged. "Sure. Aboriginal folk have been eating snakes and lizards for forty thousand years."

Trav eyed us both cautiously. "You're taking the piss, aren't you? Like with the pine tree?"

Billy laughed. "No, bein' serious now. For real, Travis. We eat them."

It took a little convincing, but Travis finally shook his head. "How do you cook them? And aren't they all bone?"

Just then, Trudy came out the back door. She looked tired still and her hair was all flat on one side, but at least she'd slept a bit. "Here's my girl," she said, taking Grace off Trav.

"Sleep okay?" I asked.

"Like the dead. Must have needed it more than I realised," she replied.

"We'll babysit any time you like," Travis said. "Me and Charlie will, that is. She was great company. Uncle Billy was just telling us how he cooks and eats snakes."

Trudy nodded slowly and walked down the steps. "Thanks for the offer. I'll take you guys up on that." As she got closer to the tree with my dead-snake-tinsel she called out, "Hey Trav?"

"Yeah?"

Trudy didn't turn around. She just kept on walking and replied, "They're bullshitting you again."

Travis looked at me, then at Billy, and Billy cracked up laughing.

"God, I hate you both." He put both hands on his hips. "You don't eat them at all."

"Some people do," Billy said, his usual half-face grin lit up. "But I prefer steak. Or Macca's."

Travis looked at me. "I expect you to be on my side."

"What?" I feigned innocence. I'm thinkin' my smile didn't help none. "He could totally eat a McSnake burger."

"I hate you so much right now." Trav stomped back inside, the screen door slamin' behind him. "I'll never believe another word you say."

"Not even if I told you I have a Christmas surprise for ya?"

His reply came from somewhere in the house. "Nuh."

MAYBE I PUSHED him too far. Maybe he still wasn't feeling great, or maybe he was still pissed over the snake thing, because he was quiet after that. Even after dinner when the house was all quiet, I pulled Trav into the lounge room, he was still out of sorts. "Okay I lied. I do have one Christmas tradition," I said.

"Yeah, what's that?"

"Something I do every year, every Christmas Eve without fail."

One corner of his mouth pulled up. "Yeah?"

"I watch my favourite Christmas movie."

His smile died and he raised one eyebrow. "Die Hard isn't a Christmas movie, Charlie."

"Yes it is. There's Christmas carols in it."

"It's true," Ma chimed in from somewhere down the hall. "He watches it every Christmas Eve."

I started to whistle *Jingle Bells* like John McClane does, and when that didn't work, I sang it until Trav smiled. "Okay, okay, I'll watch it. Again. Please don't sing. Ever."

Not even offended, I put the DVD on and claimed the sofa first. I laid down on my side and patted the seat to show Trav where I wanted him to lie in front of me. He did, with a reluctant sigh, and we settled in to watch Die Hard.

It didn't take long before I realised Trav wasn't even watching it. He was staring at the Christmas tree. I kissed the back of his head. "You okay?"

"Mm, yeah."

I put my arm around him so he couldn't escape. "Don't lie to me, Trav. I'm sorry about before, with Billy and the snake. He was just pulling your leg. I didn't mean anything by it."

"Nah, it's not that."

"Then what is it?"

He sighed. "Dunno."

"Are you disappointed?"

He turned his face so he could see me. "In what?"

"That Christmas here is a non-event. I'm sorry we don't make no fuss over it."

He smiled a little. "It's not that... I guess it's just different here. I dunno. If I were back in Texas, we'd have family for miles and food for days. Christmas in my parents' house lasts a week."

I gave him a squeeze. "You're homesick."

"A little."

I kissed the side of his head. "Thank you for telling me."

"It doesn't mean I wanna go home, Charlie."

I laughed quietly. "I know that. I know you're here for good. We've been through enough, and I know when you said this was your home, you meant it."

"I did. I still do."

"You're allowed to be homesick, Trav. You're allowed to miss your family. It's only natural." I kissed his shoulder this time. "Maybe next year we can go and have a Texas Christmas."

He turned to face me, and with us both lyin' on the couch, that weren't the easiest of things. "You mean that?"

"Anything for you."

He closed his eyes and smiled, all content like my words fixed something inside him. "Thank you."

I kissed him, just soft and sweet, and the sound of the phone ringing kinda ruined the moment. Ma stuck her head around the doorway not a moment later. "Charlie? It's Laura."

Shit. Shit, shit, shit.

My mother, Laura, and brother, Sam, were critical in the implementation of Travis's Christmas present bein' delivered on time. If something went wrong, I'd find myself drivin' three hours to Alice Springs at midnight on Christmas Eve. Not that I wouldn't do it...

I peeled myself off the couch in a mass of arms and legs and kinda fell into the hallway. I picked up the phone. "Laura."

"Oh hi, Charlie," she replied. "Is Travis there? Can you talk?"

"Yes, and not really."

She laughed. "Right then. I'll be quick. Everything's on

time; there's been no delays from Darwin. Should be there just after five."

Relief coursed through me. "Oh, that's great. I can't thank you enough."

"It's no problem. Like I said, I've been on nightshift this week so I'm up and awake, and Sam'll keep me company while I drive. Plus I get to spend my first Christmas with you in too many years." She sounded a little emotional, and if I were bein' truthful, it made me happy to hear her say that.

"I'm looking forward to it."

"Okay, we'll see you in the morning."

"Drive safe."

"Will do. Bye, Charlie."

When she hung up, knowing Trav could hear every word I was saying, I added, "Okay, have a great Christmas. Bye."

Trav was sitting up watching John McClane kick some arse, but by the over-thinkin' line between his eyebrows, I guessed he was doing more thinking than watching. "Everything okay?" he asked.

"Yeah, Laura just wanted to say Merry Christmas. She's on some crazy nightshifts and didn't want to miss sayin' hi."

Trav looked at me kinda funny, and knowin' I couldn't lie to save myself, I flicked on the Christmas tree lights, turned off the lounge room lights, and hit the off button on the TV. I held my hand out to Trav and pulled him to his feet, and there by the lights of the Christmas tree, I kissed him.

He put his hand to my face and did that nose nudgin' thing that normally made my knees buckle. I pulled back. "Ow, Trav. My nose!"

"Oh my God, sorry," he said with a laugh. He held my

face and planted soft kisses on my cheeks, my lips, and my still-sore nose. I was just about to tell him his sorry weren't real sincere considerin' he was still smiling, but then something changed. His smile melted into something serious, and his eyes darkened with want. He kissed me again, deeper this time, and he slowly opened my mouth with his. He pushed his hips against mine and groaned into the kiss.

Jesus.

"Take me to bed, Travis," I whispered.

He took my hand and took care of me, goin' over every inch of my body, with his hands, with his mouth. I was lyin' on my stomach and he was between my legs when he pushed into me, but it didn't seem quite right. Like he felt the same, he rolled me over and had me that way instead. It was better he said, kissin' me and reminding me of love and promises, looking deep into my eyes when he made me come again.

I thought my heart might just about burst.

Afterwards when he was all sated and nuzzlin' into me, all wrapped around me, he hummed his contentment. "Mmm, merry Christmas to me."

CHAPTER SEVEN

MERRY, MERRY CHRISTMAS

I WOKE UP EARLY. Actually, I barely slept at all, maybe three hours at the most. But I was up annoying Nugget at four thirty, putting presents under the Christmas tree, pacing the lounge room, waiting, waiting, waiting.

Finally—*finally*—headlights came down the drive.

My heart was in my throat, and I was prayin' that Trav wouldn't wake up when he heard the car or the voices that followed. I shouldn't have worried though, because he was sleepin' so hard, not even the smell of coffee under his nose half an hour later woke him up.

I put the cup on the side table and climbed onto the bed. Now if it were any other day, I'd watch him and the way moonlight touched his face like it were my favourite thing. Because it was.

But not today.

"Trav. Wake up."

"Mm mm," he mumbled. "Sleep in."

"You can't. It's pressies time."

He cracked one eye open. His voice was thick with sleep. "Pressies? What the hell are pressies?"

"Presents. You know, gifts."

He scrubbed his hands over his face. "Australians really shorten the word presents?"

"Well, yeah."

"Why? It takes just as much effort to say pressies as it does to say presents. There's the same amount of syllables."

I snorted. "Come on. I need you to get up."

"Why?" he grumbled. He sat up and noticed the window. "The sun ain't even freakin' up, Charlie. What the hell time is it?" he asked.

"It's just after five o'clock. It's gettin' up time."

He glared at me. "You're serious." He fell back onto the bed and pulled a pillow over his face. "Ya know, if Christmas is no big deal, it can be no big deal after six freakin' a.m."

I threw his shorts on the bed. "Hurry up, Trav. I made you coffee. The fancy stuff, not the instant powder stuff."

He pulled the pillow down. "What have you done?"

I grinned. He was gonna shit bricks. "Come on, get up. Trudy and Gracie have been up for a while. Bacon's just joined 'em. Nara and Billy are on their way." I heard voices down the hall. "That's them. Come on, Trav. We're waitin' on you."

He looked at me for three long not-speakin' seconds before he threw back the covers and grumbled the whole time he was pullin' on his shorts. I handed him his coffee and took his other hand and all but dragged him out to the lounge room. Everyone was there, kinda bleary eyed but smilin', all sitting around the lounge room lookin' at the presents under the tree. They were watching Travis, knowing what was waiting for him in the kitchen.

He sat on the lounge and sipped his coffee, still half asleep and grumbling, and I stood in front of the tree.

"Thank you all for being here this early," I said. My heart was in my throat. "Merry Christmas, everyone. I know we've never really done Christmas here before, but this year is different. Everything's different now..." I swallowed hard. "So without wasting any more time, I want to give Travis his Christmas present first."

Travis looked confused, all bleary-eyed and sleep-messed hair, and it was then Travis noticed the presents under the tree. Or more specifically, he noticed there were about twenty wrapped gifts that weren't there last night. He stared at me. "You said there were no presents." His stare became a scowl. "You told me no presents. You said we don't do presents. You made that rule, and now you're telling me you got me something?"

"Well—"

"Jesus Christ, Charlie." He was mad. "I mean I got you something, but it's only little and it didn't cost me anything because you said *no gifts!*"

"Well, what I meant was you didn't have to get me anything," I said quickly. His jaw bulged and his nostrils flared. Well, apparently that wasn't the right answer. I cringed. "Just put your coffee down and close your eyes. Please."

He didn't move. He just did that still-pissed, staring-without-speaking thing.

Ma, who was sitting next to him, took his coffee from him. "I'll take that."

"You know what it is," he mumbled, looking at Ma. Then he saw everyone was smiling. "You all know what it is." His gaze shot to mine. "What have you done?"

"Close your eyes."

I waited until he'd put his hands over his face, mumbling words I couldn't hear. I dashed off to the kitchen and came back with his present in tow. Unable to stop from grinning, I took a deep breath. "Okay. Open your eyes."

He did.

The moment he saw his mum and dad, he instantly teared up, and he jumped out of his seat, almost tackling his parents through the door.

Mr and Mrs Craig had flown from Texas to spend Christmas with their son. Actually, I'd paid to fly them out. It was my present to Travis.

"Oh my God," he said, letting his parents go so he could hug his mum then his dad in turn. He bounced, like he wasn't sure what to do with his hands and wiped his tears. "Oh my God."

Then he looked at me. "You did this?" I nodded, but before I could say anything, he hugged me too. "I hate you so much right now," he mumbled into my neck, which made me laugh. He let go of me and hugged his mum again. She was still crying. It was like Trav couldn't keep still. "How did this happen?"

Mrs Craig said, "Well, it was Charlie's idea. He phoned us up a few weeks ago and asked us if we'd like to visit."

"It was a long flight," his dad said. "Feels like we left three days ago."

Mrs Craig wiped her face and added, "We *did* leave three days ago."

"We flew into Darwin last night at some ungodly hour," Mr Craig explained, then into Alice Springs, where Charlie's mother Laura and Sam kindly drove us out here. I have to admit, Travis, I thought you were exaggerating when you said you were three hours from the closest town."

Trav looked around the room. "Laura and Sam are here?"

Laura was leaning against the hall doorway, and Sam,

who was standing behind her, gave him a wave. "Merry Christmas, Travis."

So of course, he hugged them too. "You drove them out here at midnight? After you called here last night to say you were working..." Travis spun to look at me. "You're the worst liar."

I laughed. "I kept this from you just fine."

He put his hands to my face, and in front of everyone, he kissed me.

Ma cleared her throat. "Right then. Everyone else's presents?"

Within ten minutes, everyone had opened their gifts. There was fishing gear, books, clothes, and wrapping paper everywhere. But the very best gift was the laughter. I was beginning to see why Trav liked to make a thing of Christmas.

I got a rocking horse for Gracie. I explained she was too little for it yet, but she'd grow into it, just in time for next Christmas when I got her a real pony. I ignored the death-stares from Trudy and the eye-rollin' from Bacon, and figured now probably wasn't the best time to tell them I'd already started lookin' for the perfect pony.

Travis handed me a box with a Christmas bow. "This is your non-gift. Which pales in comparison really rather spectacularly compared to your non-gift, I just have to say."

I opened my present with a stupid grin on my face that died when I saw what it was. Inside was the old photograph of my dad holding a three-year-old me. It was the photo we found in the roof, along with other things my father had put away... I loved this photo. My dad was laughing at someone off camera. He looked so happy. The frame was wood and rustic and suited the age of the photo.

"It's nothing much," Travis said.

I swallowed hard. "It's perfect."

"George helped me make the frame. There was some old palings in the shed and a sheet of glass I cleaned up. I oiled the wood and it didn't come up too bad." Trav shrugged. "I wanted you to remember him smiling like that," he said quietly.

In the last year, I'd let go of a lot of resentment toward my father. Travis was the sole reason for that. So a photo of my old man in a frame made by Travis and George from old bits and pieces from this farm made to be something new again was just about as fitting as a gift could get. "Trav, it really is perfect," I whispered, blinking back tears.

Trav pulled me in for a hug. He kissed the side of my head. "Love you, Charlie."

I put the frame on the mantelpiece, because part of me hoped my father could somehow look around the lounge room and see what a different home Sutton Station was now. I slid my hand over Travis's and gave his fingers a squeeze. "Love you too, Trav."

***

WE TALKED THE MORNING AWAY, over breakfast, and then morning tea. But Laura claimed the week of night-shifts had caught up with her, so she went to get some sleep. Sam crashed on the couch for a bit and woke up in time for lunch.

I could tell Travis's parents were beat, but they were excited and hadn't stopped talking to Trav or stopped touching him yet. It was like they could barely believe they were actually seeing him.

As the afternoon wore on and the back of the home-stead fell into shade, we all sat out the back. The cooler breeze was a godsend and made for good weather for a game of backyard cricket. Ernie and Billy, Bacon and George, and me, Sam, and Trav played, making The Three Stooges look boring, while everyone else looked on, but by God we laughed.

Ma and Nara had outdone themselves with the food. It was a real Australian Christmas dinner. There was honey-glazed baked ham, salads, and fresh-baked breads, and as the sun was setting, we had tea and scones with homemade jam and cream and a berry Pavlova for dessert.

It was pretty much perfect.

Travis's mum, Laura, and Ma talked and talked, and Mr Craig and George talked farming, making plans for their week-long stay. Nugget rolled and did burn-outs in the dirt while me and Trav kicked back with our bare feet up. We watched our families all laughing and smiling, and he took hold of my hand. "I thought you said you didn't do anything special for Christmas."

"We don't normally. Nothing fancy anyway. Just this."

"Charlie, this right here is perfect."

"I was just thinking the same thing."

"Why did you do it?" he asked. "Fly my parents out here?"

"Remember on December first, you asked about putting up a Christmas tree? And I kinda laughed, because well, we haven't done that in years."

"Yeah."

"Well, your face... you were disappointed. You tried to hide it and you acted like you didn't care, but I could tell you did."

"You flew my parents here from the States because I looked disappointed?"

I nodded. "Yep. I never want to disappoint you, Travis,"

I said quietly. "And doin' stuff to make your partner happy is what being in a relationship is all about, yeah? And it was your first Christmas here. I wanted you to be happy. That's all."

He gave me that God-I-love-you look. He leaned in close, so only I could hear him speak. "Charlie, just so you know, you're getting *so* lucky tonight."

It made me laugh. "Merry Christmas to me."

He smiled and sat back in his chair, keepin' a hold of my hand. He watched his momma laugh at something Ma said, and Trav let out one of his contented sighs. "I think this is my best Christmas yet."

"Mine too, Trav." He really had no idea just how true it was. "Mine too." *Merry Christmas to me, indeed.*

~The End.

RED DIRT IMAGO

N.R. WALKER

Red DIRT HEART IMAGO

When Charlie Sutton's neighbour Greg is notified by the Queensland government that they intend to run a pipeline through his property, Charlie vows to help him fight it. Then Travis remembers seeing butterflies at the creek near their joining fence line - the same butterflies they couldn't find in any Australian butterfly book. Hopeful this might be their only chance to stop the development, they seek the help of a specialist.

Lawson Brighton-Gale receives an email request to identify a butterfly in the Outback, only to discover it's not an Australian butterfly at all. But that's not all he discovers. The name on the request is familiar to Jack. An old friend from his university days, who also happened to be his old friend with benefits, Charlie Sutton.

Years ago, two out-of-towners met at the University of Sydney. Both studying environmental sciences, both hundreds of miles from home, and both finding their worlds open to new experiences, they fell into bed together. Meeting again after all this time, in front of Lawson and Travis, won't be awkward at all, right? Lawson and Jack's trip to Sutton Station certainly doesn't go to plan, and what they take back to Tasmania isn't just butterflies, but a cocoon of possibilities.

~ A Red Dirt Heart and Imago crossover ~
The story of when red dirt and butterflies collide.

TRAVIS and I sat at Greg Pietersen's dining table along with Greg, his wife, Jenny, and Alan, Greg's neighbour to the north.

I was Greg's closest neighbour to the west, and over the years, Greg and Alan had become both friends and allies. They were the reason I was on the Board of the Territory's Beef Farmers Association, and together the three of us were, apparently, the faces of Farming the Future in the Northern Territory.

Greg had been a mate to my old man too, and he'd been the one to come help look for Travis when Trav'd found himself lost overnight in the desert. So one phone call from him was all it took for Trav and me to be sittin' there over a cuppa with our serious faces on.

"It's bullshit," Jenny said. "They can't just do what they damn well please."

Greg gave his wife a smile. "Seems the government can do what they please, love."

I stared at the letter on the table while chewin' on my lip, tryin' to think.

"It doesn't belong to anyone," Alan added. "The Artesian Basin is an underground water supply that feeds half the Territory and Queensland into New South Wales, even South Australia. It's not theirs to take."

"The water don't belong to anyone," Greg agreed. "But the property they wanna run a pipeline through certainly does."

No one spoke for a bit, while we all let our tempers simmer down and our thoughts settle into order. The thing was, I was really pissed about this. No, the bloody government hadn't declared they'd just drop a few hundred kilometres of pipeline through Sutton Station, but they did tell Greg they'd put it through his place. And that was something I just couldn't rightly let happen.

I would defend his property like it was my own.

"Have you spoken to Melville?" I asked. Melville owned property to the north of Greg, and he was no friend of mine.

Greg's eyes met mine, and he shook his head in disgust. "The old bastard's happy to sell it off. His kids don't want his place, and he can't work it like he should. I reckon he was as happy as a pig in the proverbial when he got his letter."

I had to unclench my jaw so I could speak. "I wouldn't be surprised."

Greg's nostrils flared. "I don't want their bloody money, not a goddamn cent. What they're proposin' to pay us off with isn't worth shit anyway."

"Then we fight them," Alan said. "In court. The Supreme Court if we have to."

"They'll just wait us out to bleed us dry," Greg mumbled. I'd never seen him so resigned, like he was beat already. "They'll be expecting that and'll simply tie us up in red tape until we can't afford to stay."

I shook my head. "This ain't over yet. Not by a long shot." I tapped the table with my finger. "It'll be a cold day in hell when I let some pen-pushin' government idiot tell me what they will and won't do with my land, and I sure as shit won't let 'em tell you what they're gonna do with yours."

Jenny squeezed Greg's hand, and I gave her a smile. I could hear their boys playin' in the room next door, and I could only imagine what trouble Milly was getting' up to at home with Ma.

I lifted my chin and set my jaw. My mind was made up. "Jenny's right," I said. "It is bullshit, and they won't do what they damn well please. This is our land, this is our kids' land, and it'll be over my dead body that they try and take anythin' away from my daughter."

Greg smiled properly for the first time all day. "There's the Sutton I know."

I noticed Trav then, staring out the window like he was a million miles away. He had that busy-thinkin' line between his eyebrows. "Whatcha reckon, Trav? We'll find some way to fight 'em, yeah?"

Trav looked right at me. "Absolutely. Oh, we'll fight them all right." Then he sat forward in his seat and stared right at me, his blue eyes as intense as I'd ever seen 'em. "Charlie, you remember the other week we were out fixing fences along the northwestern paddock? What did we see in that creek that I couldn't find in no book?"

I nodded. "Yeah, I remember." Then I clued in to what he was getting at, and I began smiling. I turned to Greg. "If we're gonna fight these bastards, then we need to beat 'em at their own game. And I reckon Trav might've just figured out how."

"JACK?" I'd just opened and read an email that was quite interesting. I picked up my laptop and closed up the butterfly house, going in search of Jack. It was a Sunday, and he'd been busy tending to the gardens and pottering around while I was holed up in my lab. I found him in the kitchen, slicing apple and cheese, one of his favourite snacks for TV watching. "Oh, there you are."

"Hey," he said with a smile. He looked at my laptop. "What's up?"

"I just received an email from Piers Bonfils."

"Oh, how's he going? The Ulysses still breeding okay?" He held a small slice of apple to my lips, which I took into my mouth. Then he frowned. "It is okay, isn't it? The Ulysses, it's not dying again, is it?"

I finished chewing the apple and swallowed. "Oh no, all is well in that regard."

Jack slid some crackers straight from the box onto the plate of apple and cheese. Then he tossed a small square of cheese into his mouth. "So, what's up?"

"There's a fellow who wanted help identifying a butterfly. He took photographs and sent them to Piers. Piers confirmed it was definitely worth looking into, but he was simply too busy with the Ulysses, so he recommended me." I turned the laptop around and showed Jack the photograph. "It's a *Charaxes brutus*, the White-barred Emperor, by the look of it. Very remarkable."

He studied the picture for a moment, then me. "Is it endangered?"

"It is on a watch list, but that's not what makes it remarkable."

He raised an eyebrow. "What makes it remarkable?"

"Because it's only found in Africa."

Jack's eyes widened. "Africa? He wants you to go to *Africa*?"

I smiled at him. Lord knows, he was probably envisioning me being eaten by a lion or hippo. "No, the Northern Territory."

"Oh." He huffed out a breath in relief. Then he mumbled, "Thank God for that."

I ignored that and went back to the email. "Do you know a Charlie Sutton?"

Jack choked on a piece of cheese.

How odd.

"Are you all right?" I patted him on the back.

"Yeah, yeah," he said, swallowing hard. "That's just a name I haven't heard in a long time."

"Well, I take it you do know him. May I ask how?"

He nodded slowly. "We went to uni together."

"And you were sexual partners," I deduced. "Your reaction said enough."

Jack made a face and went a little red. "Well, yes, but that was a long time ago. We were at uni. You know how that is."

I chuckled at his horrified expression and stole another piece of his apple. "Well, yes. You have no reason to worry, Jack. Or to be embarrassed."

"It just kind of came from nowhere," he said, back under control now. "Remember when we were in Cairns that time at the CSIRO building and I sat in the waiting room and was reading a magazine article? I said it was of a guy I went to uni with. Well, that was him. Some big-shot farmer he is now. Well, he was. That magazine was a few years old even back then."

"I think I remember that," I answered, when the truth was, I hadn't a clue.

Then a look of confusion crossed Jack's features. "If the email is from Piers, what on earth does Charlie Sutton have to do with anything?"

"The butterfly was found on or near his property."

Jack gave a piece of cheese to the patiently waiting Rosemary. "Oh. The African butterfly?"

I nodded and smiled at the idea of going on another butterfly hunting expedition. "What are the chances of you taking some time off work for an Outback adventure?"

"Well, if you think I'd let you wander off on your own into the desert where the deadliest snakes in the world call home, you've got another thing coming."

I resisted the urge to roll my eyes. Barely. "Not forgetting the fact I'll be meeting a man who you've slept with."

Jack pouted, most adorably. "That too."

"Excellent. I'll reply in the affirmative, yes?"

"Uh, I guess."

I sat myself on the sofa with my laptop and replied to Piers. By the time Jack sat down beside me with his plate of snacks and two glasses of wine, I'd already had a response. I took the offered wine glass and gave him a grateful smile. "I have contact details. Piers said this Charlie fellow said it was urgent. Should I call him now?"

Jack bit his lip and nodded, so I took out my mobile and called the number in the email. It answered on the third ring. "Hello? Sutton Station," an older female voice said.

"Yes, good afternoon. My name is Lawson Brighton-Gale. I was hoping to speak to a Mr Charlie Sutton."

"Can I ask what it's about? If you're selling something, I'll save us all some time and stop you right there."

I almost laughed. "No, I'm not selling anything. I'm a lepidopterist."

Silence.

So I elaborated. "I'm calling about the butterflies."

"Oh! Oh, sorry, yes, he'd be real interested in speaking with you. Please just hold on and I'll go find him. He was out the back." There was a dull clunking noise followed by the sound of a screen door slamming, then a faint, "Charlie! It's a man about the butterflies!" Then silence for a short while, more footsteps, and then a gruff, warm voice spoke into the phone. "Hello, this is Charlie Sutton."

I smiled at Jack. "Hello, Mr Sutton. My name is Lawson Brighton-Gale. I have received your email from the Cairns Butterfly Conservatory. Professor Piers Bonfils thought I might be able to offer some assistance."

"Ah, yeah, we found a kind of butterfly we couldn't find in no book, and we were hoping it was some kind of new or endangered species?"

"Well, from what I can assess by the one photograph, if it's the butterfly I'm thinking it is, it's neither new nor endangered."

"Oh." He sounded disappointed.

"But there's never been one found in Australia, Mr Sutton."

"Really?"

"Yes. From the one picture, I would be confident enough to name it. Though I was hoping you would have more photographs you could send me. I'd like to determine if it is indeed a White-barred Emperor before I trek a few thousand kilometres to see it for myself."

"Oh sure!" He was excited now and talking to someone else, asking them about the photos. I gave him my email address, and as we waited for them to arrive in my inbox, he asked, "So, you'd need to come out and take a look?"

"Yes. Is that a problem?"

"No, no, not at all. If it is one of those White Emperors—"

"White-barred Emperor," I corrected.

"Right. If it is one of those, then what happens next?"

"I would confer with the Lepidopterist Society of Australia."

"And?"

Hmm. "Mr Sutton, may I ask why the urgency? You're very keen for this finding to be in your favour."

It sounded as though he ran his hand over his face. "I'm gonna be honest with ya, Mr Brighton-Gale. We're running outta time. Ya see, the government wants to run a pipeline through my neighbour's place, right where we found these butterflies. Or close enough to 'em. And we were hopin' if these butterflies were special enough, it just might stop the pipeline."

Just then, my laptop pinged with an email from Sutton Station. I clicked on the attached photographs. "I've just received the photos," I said, in case Mr Sutton was beginning to question my silence.

The pictures weren't perfect, but I could see enough. The butterfly itself looked like a *Charaxes brutus*, though I was more interested in seeing what plant the butterfly was on. That would tell me more. I pointed to the green foliage on screen and looked at Jack. "What kind of plant is that?"

He studied the photo for a moment, squinting and frowning. "It looks like *Grewia insularis*. It's a species of flowering plant in the *Malvaceae* family, but I'd need better photos to be sure."

I didn't really need to know any more. If there was a White-barred Emperor in Australia, the only type of plant the caterpillar would feed upon was the *Grewia insularis*.

"Mr Sutton, those specific plants in the photograph, do you have those anywhere else on your property?"

"No, we don't. Not that I've seen. These were along a creek on Greg's property. We were fixin' fences and stopped to water the horses when Travis saw them. The butterflies, that is. That's when he saw the *butterflies*. They're kinda big, and we thought they were little birds at first, so he took some photos, and when we got home, he couldn't find them in any Australian butterfly books."

"Because they're not Australian. They're African. And Mr Sutton, if you're agreeable, I'd like to come and see them for myself."

"That'd be real great, Mr Brighton-Gale."

"I should tell you now, I'll be bringing my husband along with me."

A brief pause. "Husband?"

"Yes. Is that a problem?"

He snorted into the phone, then laughed. "Uh no. No problem at all."

"Good. Because I believe you know him. His name is Jack Brighton."

CHAPTER THREE

CHARLIE

JACK BRIGHTON? Well, holy shit. That's a name I hadn't thought of in a hundred years. After we'd exchanged contact details and the butterfly guy had told me he'd be in touch when they were coming, I called Greg to let him know what was happening. Then it was dinner time, then bath and bedtime for Milly, and by the time we were ready to hit the hay ourselves, I still hadn't told Travis.

"What is it, Charlie?" he asked after I closed our bedroom door. He was sittin' on the edge of our bed, all long-legged-like, with a smug smile. "I know you've got something you don't want to tell me."

I leaned against the bedroom door and sighed. "It's about the butterfly guy."

"What about him?"

"Actually, it's about his husband?"

"He's gay?"

"Well, I dunno. But he's married to a guy, so he ain't exactly straight, Trav."

Travis chuckled. "Fair enough. What about his husband?"

"I know him."

"So?"

"From Sydney. We went to uni together. A lot, if you know what I mean..."

I could see the second he put the pieces together. Me. Sydney. Uni. He'd once said my uni days sounded like I'd slept with the entire gay population of Sydney, and I'd joked that I thought some were possibly straight... Yeah, that kind of we-went-to-uni-together.

Travis raised one of his eyebrows in a perfect arch. "A lot?"

I cringed. "There weren't many that were repeats, if you know what I mean. But he was one of them."

"One of the guys you slept with *a lot* when you were at uni is coming here? With his husband?"

I frowned and nodded. *God, this was a bad idea.*

Travis stared at me for a good long second before he busted up laughing. He laughed so hard he fell back on the bed, and then he laughed some more.

I stalked over to him and knelt on the bed so I was straddlin' his thighs. "It's not that funny, Trav."

He could hardly speak he was laughing so hard. "Oh my God, Charlie. It's hilarious."

I poked at his chest. "It's not funny. It's embarrassing. They're coming here, and it's gonna be awkward as hell."

He waggled his eyebrows and grinned. "Maybe his husband'll suggest a foursome?"

I took a hold of his hands and roughly pinned them to the mattress above his head and leaned down so my nose was almost touching his. His eyes were full of mischief and heat. "No one touches you but me. And the only man who'll ever touch me is you."

He hummed. "I do love it when you get all possessive."

Still pinnin' his hands to the bed, I rearranged us so I could spread his legs with my knees. I rocked into him, our jeans makin' the most delicious friction. "How possessive do you want me to get?"

Trav grinned like he'd won first prize. "I want you to ride me like you stole me, Charlie."

I laughed and kissed him when there was a tiny knock on our bedroom door. Not tiny-soundin', but tiny as in the hands that did the knockin'.

I bit back a groan and climbed off the bed. Before I opened the door, I did a double-check that me and Trav were both respectable enough for innocent eyes. I pulled back the door to find Milly in her PJ's, her reddish, copper-coloured hair in loose curls down her shoulders, and her offsider in her arms. "What's up, pumpkin?"

Milly looked up at me with her huge brown eyes. "Nugget can't sleep."

I looked at the wombat. He blinked at me, did his nose-twitchin' thing, and I swear the little bugger smiled. "Are you sure it's Nugget that can't sleep?"

Milly nodded.

"Want me to read him a story?" I asked.

She grinned, just like the one Trav'd given me earlier, and ran into our room. She barrelled up onto the bed, never letting go of Nugget, and landed herself right in the middle of our pillows. Milly grinned. Nugget grinned. I sighed, and Travis laughed.

"What about your bed?" I asked. "I'm pretty sure four-year-olds are old enough for stories in their own beds."

Milly just snuggled down and pulled the blankets over Nugget. They both looked at me expectantly. Waiting. Nose-twitching. Smiling.

It was hard to be mad when she was so stinkin' cute. "Okay, Milly-moo. Which book?"

Trav walked out with his pyjamas in his hand, smiling from ear to ear. And so, instead of one-on-one daddy time, the four of us—me, Trav, Milly, and Nugget—spent the next hour reading *A Wombat's Diary* fifty-seven times.

Now, I know it's not the same as bein' intimate with my husband, and that was something I'd truly never tire of, but nights spent in bed reading picture books to a giggling gorgeous girl and a snuffling, wiggling wombat would forever be my favourite.

Trav carried a sound asleep Milly back to her bed, and I took a disgruntled Nugget, who burrowed right back in beside her when I put him in her bed. Some kids had a teddy bear or a blankey. Milly had a Nugget.

Trav leaned in and kissed her forehead, I turned out the lights and closed the door as quiet as I could. Ya know, in all my years of sneakin' in around Ma tryin' to get away with shit I shouldn't have been getting' away with, I never did know the art of bein' quiet until Milly was born.

Puttin' her down to sleep was like puttin' a ticking bomb to bed. Trav was always better at it than me; those big skilled hands of his could carry a glass grenade without breakin' a sweat.

We tiptoed back to our room and Trav closed the door and both of us breathed in relief. He took my face in his hands and kissed me with smiling lips. "She's the most precious thing, but damn, how can she not need sleep?"

I pulled off my shirt, then undid my jeans and kicked 'em into the hamper in the corner. It was late now, and the playful mood between me and Trav had simmered to a quiet, sleepy air instead. And that was okay too.

We climbed into bed, and I found my comfy spot

nestled right into Travis' side, his arm around my shoulder, my face on his chest. "So," he started before pressing a kiss to the top of my head. "What's the plan with the butterfly guys?"

"Well, I told them we were outta time, so they said they can get here on the weekend."

"Wow, that's fast."

"Yeah, hopefully they can identify the butterfly and get whatever paperwork they need to get done so Greg can stop the pipeline."

Travis gave me a squeeze. "Let's hope so." We were quiet a while and my eyelids and mind were heavy with sleepin'. "Do you reckon we'll need to camp out with them?"

"I already pre-warned George and Ma we might need to do that, yeah."

"For how long, do you reckon?"

"Dunno. How long does it take to find a butterfly? Didn't take you long."

His chest vibrated as he laughed. "It'll be getting colder soon. Means campfires and joined sleeping bags."

I smiled and sighed as Trav's arms tightened around me. "Sounds good."

"Do you reckon the butterfly guy and your ex'll mind if we get some personal time in while we're camp-side?"

I snorted. "He's not my ex. We were never... like that."

"Friends with benefits?"

"Barely even friends. Just... benefits."

Travis chuckled and kissed the top of my head. "I'm looking forward to meeting him."

I put my head up so I could see his face. "Does it bother you? That someone I've had... benefits with will be here?"

Trav just shook his head and grinned. "It's my ring on

your finger, Charlie. It's our daughter asleep down the hall, and it's me you beg for and my name you whisper." He sighed, content and sleepy. His accent was always thicker when he was tired. "I know damn well who you belong to. And you do too."

CHAPTER FOUR

JACK BRIGHTON-GALE

I'D NEVER BEEN to Alice Springs before, and from the view out the aeroplane window, it looked very red and flat. Not to say that it wasn't beautiful, I'd just never seen anything like it. Red, red dirt stretched flat to the horizon in every direction.

We collected all of Lawson's research gear from the airport cargo, signed for everything, collected the rental—which was a Defender, of course—and called ahead to Sutton Station. We let them know we'd arrived and were heading straight out so they could expect us in three hours.

Who the hell lived three hours from the nearest town? *God.* No wonder Charlie ran amok when he got to Sydney.

I drove, following the GPS directions, which admittedly said as much as 'turn right onto the Plenty Highway and follow for three hundred kilometres.' Lawson did some more reading up on the African White-barred Emperor butterfly. When I slowed down to turn into a driveway with a sign marked Sutton Station, Lawson shut his iPad off and looked out the window.

"Wow."

I chuckled. "It's strangely beautiful, isn't it?"

He nodded. "I thought our house was isolated."

That made me laugh. "Our ten acres wouldn't be a speck out here."

After a while, Lawson looked at the GPS. "Did you take a wrong turn? I thought he said his driveway was directly off the highway."

"This *is* his driveway."

He peered out at the isolation. "Good Lord."

In the distance I could see a patch of green trees and finally some sign of life in the form of a manmade building, which as we got closer, I could see were actually several buildings. A house, some sheds, stables, water tanks.

It was strange to feel a little nervous. We'd tried to search Charlie Sutton online, and while there were many posts on his business and farming acumen, his position on some Territory Beef Farmers board, and a few photographs to go with those sites, there was nothing on his private life.

I had no clue what to expect.

I pulled the four-wheel drive up at the house and took a deep breath. It was a nice looking farmhouse, with a front veranda and a bullnose roof. It looked well lived in and very well loved. "Well, this is it."

Lawson gave me a quick smile and opened his door, so I did the same. Just as I was getting out, the front door of the house opened and a man walked out. He wore faded jeans, an old KingGee shirt, boots, a hat that was more holes than hat, and a smile I recognised immediately.

Charlie Sutton.

He came down the steps and crossed the small lawn area and stuck out his hand as he walked. "Jack," he said. "Long time, mate."

"Charlie." I shook his hand. His hands were as hard as

his grip, calloused and warm. By this time, Lawson was beside us. "Charlie, this is my husband, Lawson."

Charlie offered him the same smile he gave me, and Lawson shook his hand. "Nice to meet you. Thank you for having us."

"Thank you for comin'," Charlie said. "How was your flight? Makes for a long day, yeah?"

"Yeah," I answered. "Left Launceston at six this morning." I checked my watch. It was almost four in the afternoon. "The flight was fine, and the drive out here was prettier than expected."

Charlie was just smiling at me like it was good to see me. Then he clapped his hands together. "Right, let's get your things inside and I'll show you to your room."

Just then, a young lady appeared and Charlie introduced her as Nara. We all said our hellos, and without prompting, she helped herself to taking our luggage and Lawson's research tubs. They probably could have stayed in the rental, but Lawson always liked to double check everything, so we hauled them inside too. "Milly won't put pants on," Nara said to Charlie. He sighed but nodded like he expected nothing less. And I wondered idly if this Nara was Charlie's wife. Just because he slept with guys didn't mean he couldn't fancy women as well. And then I wondered who the hell Milly was and why she was opposed to pants.

Charlie pulled out a suitcase, looked at us, and grinned. "It's a madhouse here some days. Come on in."

The house itself was beautiful. Old wooden floors and traditional wood panelled walls painted white. This house had history and warmth and felt like a home. Charlie showed us to a spare room, with a double bed and a stand-alone wardrobe and dresser, and a window with a light curtain blowing in the breeze. Nara had already put the tubs in the corner, so we dumped our belongings as well and followed Charlie back out to the living room, where an older woman met us. "This is Ma. She's the boss."

She wiped her hands on her apron before offering to shake hands. "So nice to meet you. And I'm not really the boss. Charlie is, but—"

"But he does what she says. We all do," said an older man as he walked in. "George," he declared himself to be. He had a slow meandering way about him, a kind smile, and a strong, weathered handshake.

Then a door shut somewhere, followed by quick footsteps, a weird scratching sound, and laughter. We all turned to the hallway just in time to see a young girl with long reddish-brown hair running in but getting grabbed and hauled up onto the shoulder of a blond man. She squealed in delight just as Charlie darted to the side and caught what at first I thought was a football. But it had little scurrying legs, huge claws, and it snuffled and snorted. "No you don't, you little..." Charlie said as he wrestled with it, and when he uprighted it in his arms, I could see he was holding a wombat.

Then I looked back at the man holding the girl. He was a very handsome man, tall with striking blue eyes and a huge smile. "Sorry about that," he said with an American accent. "I've been trying to get her dressed and her hair brushed since lunchtime."

He held out his hand, but it was Charlie who made the introductions. "This is my husband, Travis."

Husband? So he married too, huh?

"Trav, this is Jack." I shook his hand and ignored the knowing smirk he gave me. "And this is Lawson."

Travis shook Lawson's hand too, then put the little girl down, but held onto her shoulders. "And this is Milly.

Milly, who is wearing a tutu because she refused to wear anything else, and I only pick the battles I can win."

Milly looked up at me, then at Lawson. She had a cherub's face, with huge brown eyes. "Hello."

"Hello," Lawson and I said together.

"My name is 'Melia Sutton," she replied, smarter than her years, no doubt. "And Daddy's got my Nugget."

Charlie held up the wombat. "This would be her partner in crime." The wombat blinked and snuffled. "Or as we like to call them, Seek and Destroy."

Wait... *Charlie's a father?*

Milly put her hands up to Charlie and he gently handed the wombat over. Milly held onto him dearly.

"May I pat him?" Lawson asked. "He sure is cute."

Milly nodded, and Lawson crouched down, so he was more on their level, and scratched Nugget on the forehead. "Why do you wear that?" Milly asked, nodding to Lawson's bow tie.

"It's a bow tie."

She smiled. "It looks like a butterfly."

"It does," Lawson agreed with a laugh.

Her eyes got really big as she remembered something. "You will look for the butterflies?"

Lawson nodded. "Yes, I will."

"Do you catch them?"

"Sometimes."

"I catch lizards. Sometimes their tails fall off."

Lawson fought a smile. "Do you keep them or let them go?"

"Daddy makes me let them go. I feed them bugs. Nugget eats apples and carrots and does square poop."

Everyone stifled their laughter. Travis put his hand on

Milly's shoulder. "Milly, honey, why don't you go put Nugget to bed and wash your hands."

"But Dada…"

Dada? If Charlie's her Daddy, and Travis is her Dada…

"No buts."

Travis must have used a tone she knew wasn't good to argue with because she pouted and walked out of the room.

"Sorry about that," Charlie said. "Like I said, it's a madhouse some days."

"It's all right," Lawson said. "She's positively adorable."

Charlie snorted. "Yeah, well, don't be fooled. She's as pigheaded as—"

"As you, Charlie," Ma finished for him. Then she smiled at us. "Now, I'm about to start dinner. You boys eat everything?"

"Everything," I replied.

"Is there anything we can do to help?" Lawson asked.

Ma looked at us like that was funny, and George snorted. "Only if you got a death wish, son." Charlie grinned and Travis laughed.

"Thank you, but if I need help, I'll be sure to ask for it," Ma said, giving us a wink before she disappeared. George followed her, leaving Lawson and me with Charlie and Travis.

"We're both her fathers," Charlie said to me. "I could see you tryin' to figure it out."

I felt myself blush a little. "I uh, I wasn't sure. But wow. Fatherhood, huh?"

"It's been a helluva road," Charlie said, giving Travis a smile. "But there ain't nothin' like it."

"We've got a Border collie named Rosemary," I offered with a shrug.

Charlie laughed, and he seemed to study me a while. "You look good, Jack. It's been a long time."

"It has. And you too. Life's been pretty good to you, I can see."

He looked up at Travis and smiled. "Won't hear me complainin'." Then he nodded toward the front of the house. "How 'bout we take a walk. I can show you around the homestead and tell ya what we know about this butterfly."

Lawson brightened at that. "Sounds great."

As it turned out, Travis fell into step with Lawson, and Charlie and I followed. We walked toward the stables first, and Travis and Lawson were quickly talking about soil quality and filtration principles, particle ratios and something else I couldn't follow.

Charlie and I were further behind them now, and it gave us a little privacy. "Those two look like they could talk forever," I said, nodding toward our husbands.

"Trav loves talkin' science."

I chuckled. "Then he and Lawson will get along fine."

"So, been married long?"

"Two years. How about you?"

"Almost five."

"Wow."

"Yeah, happened pretty quick, considerin' I didn't think I'd ever find anyone out here."

"It's amazing what you find when you're not looking, isn't it?"

Charlie smiled, stopped walking, and looked out across the paddock. "Yes, it is. Even when it lands on your doorstep and refuses to go back to America."

I laughed. "I thought you were supposed to be the stubborn one."

His grin just got wider. "I met my match, that's for damn sure. How about you?"

"Lawson is... everything I'm not. If there was a case of opposites attract, then we'd be it. I dunno how, but it just works. We have ecology in common, natural sciences, and conservation is a passion. Our old uni professors'd be proud."

"They'd be shocked," Charlie amended with a smirk.

"You never did graduate," I mused, resting my forearms on the fence to what looked like a round yard for breaking in horses.

"Yeah, I did. I went back. Trav made me. There was no way I could leave here, so I did it by correspondence."

"That's really good, Charlie. Glad to hear that." I looked at him, then to the vast space before us. "I seem to recall you once saying you wouldn't ever come back here."

He gave me an eye-crinkling smile. "Nah. This stuff right here"—he kicked at the red dirt at our feet—"is in my blood. There's no leavin' it now."

The sound of Lawson laughing made us both turn toward him. There was Travis, doing some arm motion like he was trying to start an invisible lawnmower, and Lawson was still laughing. Charlie snorted at the sight, and he looked at his husband like he was seeing him for the first time.

Then, embarrassed, like he knew I'd caught him in a private moment, he changed subjects. "Wanna see something?"

"Sure!"

He put his fingers in his mouth and let out a helluva whistle, then looked at me and grinned. Lawson and Travis walked back, and Travis was holding two carrots, green leaves and all. He handed one to Charlie. "Don't tell Ma."

I heard them before I saw them. The sound of hooves, and Charlie climbed through the fence. Two horses came into view in a cloud of red dust, and Charlie just walked out toward them.

"Is that safe?" Lawson asked.

Travis chuckled but didn't say anything, he just watched.

The horses came in at a full gallop. Charlie raised his hand, and both horses pulled up to a stop just a metre from him. Their chests heaved, their heads bobbed, and dust swirled at their feet, and Charlie never even flinched. The taller horse, a chestnut-coloured one, stomped its foot and reared its head, snorting at him.

"Oh, that's enough outta you. Trav's got yours," Charlie said to it. Travis climbed through the fence then and was met by what I guessed was his horse.

"Hey, boy," Travis said, giving him a scratch on the forehead. He fed him the carrot and gave him a quick check over.

Charlie, on the other hand, was having a quiet word with his horse. It was much smaller, mottled in colour, and one I wouldn't exactly call pretty. "This is Harriet," Charlie said. "One of the smartest stock horses I ever saw." At first glance, I'd have said he was being patient with his horse, but the more I watched them, the more I felt it was Harriet who was being patient with Charlie. He fed her the carrot and scratched her behind the ear. She nodded in thanks.

"I'll feed them early, yeah?" Travis asked.

"May as well," Charlie answered. Then he looked at me and Lawson. "We were gonna ride out tomorrow."

A horrified Lawson opened his mouth, then snapped it shut. "Ride?"

Charlie smiled. "Well, we *were* thinkin' of it because we

just don't do it as much as we'd like, but it's not gonna work. So the plan I thought would suit us all best was Trav and I'll drive out first, you guys follow us out with your gear. Now, I dunno how long you'd be expectin' it to take, but we can camp out overnight if need be."

"How far out is the site where you located the butterfly?" Lawson asked.

"It's about three hundred kilometres east of here," Travis said. "Technically, it's on Greg's property next door to us." He led both horses into the stables.

"You'll meet Greg in the morning," Charlie said. He climbed back through the fence. "So if we leave here around six a.m., we'll get out there around nine. How does that sound?"

"Perfect," Lawson answered. "I hope you don't mind, but I have some maps and location information I'd like to go over before we leave."

Charlie nodded. "No problem. After dinner when the table's cleared away, we can take a look at whatever you need."

Lawson was pleased by this. "Excellent. And I certainly hope we find the answers you're looking for."

Charlie clapped Lawson on the shoulder as we turned to walk back to the house. "So do I."

Lawson looked at Charlie as I followed. "Would you really ride your horses for three hundred kilometres?"

"Sure. Bein' out there on horseback, just me and Travis, is... well, it's kinda like what some'd call a date night." Charlie stopped walking and looked as though he might apologise for what he just said, but instead he just shrugged. "We don't get much alone time these days, what with Milly and all."

Before Lawson could respond, the front door opened and Milly ran out. "Daddy, Ma wants you inna kitchen."

Charlie turned to me and Lawson. "Duty calls. I'll leave you two to get freshened up. I reckon dinner'll be on the table in about half an hour." Then Charlie picked Milly up and tucked her under his arm like a giggling football, and they disappeared inside.

Lawson stood there and watched them for a moment. "You okay?" I asked him quietly.

"Yes, of course." He offered a tight smile.

Then Milly appeared on the veranda again. "'Scuse me, mister," she said, looking at Lawson. "Can you show me the butterflies on my Dada's 'puter?"

He smiled genuinely at her. "I would love to." He leapt up onto the veranda beside her, and she told him how Ma and Nara didn't like the butterflies in their veggie garden as they walked inside.

I found myself smiling at the screen door when Travis came up beside me. "You good?"

"Oh, yeah, fine," I answered. "Dinner's not far away, apparently."

"Awesome." Travis gave me a high-wattage smile. "Oh, in case Charlie didn't tell you already, rule number one is don't be late for dinner. Well, there's the rules about shirts and shoes too, and cussing of course, but I don't reckon you need to worry about that."

I chuckled. "No, I don't reckon I do."

CHAPTER FIVE

TRAVIS CRAIG

I HAVE TO ADMIT, when I first met this Lawson fella, I took one look at his bow tie and perfect hair, and heard him speak all proper-like, and thought *oh boy*. Actually, my first thought was, I hope he finds this butterfly soon because he sure didn't seem the type to last long out here.

But then I got to talkin' with him when we gave Charlie and Jack some time to catch up, and it didn't take me long to figure out he was one smart cookie. And then I watched him when he was with Milly, explaining to her how butterflies did their thing. She took him to the garden out back and showed him where those plant-eating caterpillars got into Ma's veggies, and Lawson listened to her like it was the most important thing he'd heard all day.

I respected him after that.

Then after dinner, Lawson laid maps out over the table and got his iPad out, and he and Charlie went over them, marking GPS locations and talkin' topography and soil types. He had a tub of equipment he said he took with him everywhere, full of things like a barometric reading thermometer, a satellite phone, and some other gadgets. Charlie was all excited to show him the cattle tracking collars we had installed, showing him on screen that we could see wherever the herds were in any part of the 2.5-million acres we owned. Lawson was amazed, and they talked about how technology and science integration was fundamental. All the while, Jack just stood back and smiled at their entire interaction.

Now, Jack was something else entirely.

He was a big fella, and it was pretty easy to see he worked outdoors a lot. He had that natural strength that showed in his shoulders and arms. He had dark hair and a charming smile, and in that regard, he reminded me a lot of Charlie. I could see why they fell into each other's company all those years ago.

I hated to admit that I didn't particularly like knowin' this other man had experience of an intimate nature with Charlie. There might not have been any emotions involved, but Jack had been with Charlie in bed. He'd been naked with him, touched him, kissed him, tasted him. Looking between them now, I had to wonder which one of them topped. Had Charlie been the one to fuck Jack, or had Jack been inside him?

"Isn't that right, Trav?"

Huh? *Shit.* "What? Sorry, I was a million miles away." I flashed them all an apologetic smile, but I didn't think Charlie was fooled.

He tilted his head and eyed me cautiously. "I was just tellin' them of the time you came off Shelby and busted your knee up pretty bad. Spent a day and night out in the desert in the middle of summer."

"Oh, I'm glad you were found." Lawson gave Jack a look. "And it's a little reassuring that I'm not the only one who has had a run of bad luck. Though I couldn't even imagine being out here in summer. It's hot enough now in autumn."

"A run of bad luck?" Jack asked Lawson, his eyebrows near his hairline. He looked at me and Charlie and smiled as he spoke. "We've had encounters with bushfires, cane toads, sprained ankles in the Snowies, and—"

"And I don't think they need to hear any more," Lawson said, raising his chin. "I assure you, I'm most prepared when on expeditions. The cane toad poisoning was hardly my fault, and Mount Kosciuszko was simply unfortunate footing. Admittedly, the bushfire was foolish, but the Blue Mountains incident was a freak of nature, really."

Charlie chuckled. "Well, if it's any consolation, the snakes out here are gettin' ready for sleepin' at the moment, being autumn and all."

"Snakes?" Lawson gaped.

Just then, a pyjama-clad Milly appeared in the doorway with Ma. "Bath's all done," Ma said.

Charlie went over to them. "Aw, thanks, Ma. You didn't need to do that."

"My pleasure. I knew you boys'd be busy. Can I get anyone a cup of tea?"

We all said, "No, thanks," but then Lawson said, "If it's not any bother, I would love a bag of fruit scraps or rotten fruit if you have it. If not, it's fine."

Ma stared at him like he'd lost his mind. "Uh..."

"We'll need it tomorrow," Lawson explained, "for the butterflies."

"Oh. Course. I'll see what I can find." Ma gave us a nod, bid us a good night with a promise to see us bright and early.

Charlie picked Milly up, and she put her head on his shoulder, clearly tired. "Story time?" he asked her quietly.

She nodded with sleepy blinks, so Charlie gave me a smile. "Won't be long."

We all watched him leave, then Lawson asked, "Travis, may I trouble you for any more of the photographs you took of the butterfly?"

"Oh, sure. I'll just grab my laptop." I'd sent him all the ones I thought were pretty good, but if he wanted to see every photo I took before heading out there in the morning, I had no problem with that. I grabbed my laptop while Lawson and Jack folded up the maps and cleared away the table, but as I was walking back in, I found Nugget wandering the hallway, probably wondering where everyone went. I scooped him up and brought him with me. "Here," I said, handing Nugget over to Jack.

Jack was a bit surprised, and it was pretty obvious he'd never really held a baby before. Or a wombat. But he soon settled Nugget on his back, and both of them seemed happy with this arrangement. "Wow, he's heavier than he looks."

"Yeah, he's like a brick," I agreed.

"Milly picks him up like he weighs nothing."

That made me laugh. "She's never known life without him."

Jack looked at Nugget and made a thoughtful face. "How old is this little fella?"

"He'd have to be six." Jack looked surprised by that, so I explained. "He's small. The vet said he's perfectly healthy, but he's just a runt. Said it could be from when we found him; his mum was on the side of the road, been hit by a car. We don't know how long he wasn't fed for."

Jack frowned at the wombat. "But he's fine now?"

"Oh yeah. Been a pain in our ass ever since. But we wouldn't have him any other way." Then I thought about that. "Well, I coulda done without the foot-bitin' thing he had going on for a few years. But he and Milly are as thick as thieves."

Jack gave me a smile, the genuine kind that made me like him whether I wanted to or not. "They're both as cute as hell. You're very lucky."

I nodded. "We know."

"Travis," Lawson said. He'd been studying the laptop screen so long I'd almost forgot he was there. "Can I ask you about these?" He pointed to the ground in one of the photos, and we got talking about that for a while. He was probably asking questions I couldn't rightly answer to the degree he wanted, but he was getting more excited. Until he looked up at Jack, who was standing, leaning against the table, rocking a wombat to sleep in his arms, and I reckon I saw the moment Lawson melted into love all over again.

I recognised it because I'd looked at Charlie exactly the same way every time I saw him holding a newborn Milly. It was an overwhelming thing that detonated in your chest like a bomb, filling every part of your entire being with a need to love and protect.

Jack seemed to sense our eyes on him because he looked up and smiled with a shyness that belied his size. "He's almost asleep," he whispered.

Charlie appeared in the door. "Milly's finally out." Then he noticed Jack and Nugget, and he smirked. "Come through here. You can put him to bed."

Lawson and I watched them walk out, and Lawson gave me a slight smile before closing the laptop. I wondered if he was okay with meetin' Charlie or if he had the same trepidation I had about Jack. I didn't know why I felt such jealousy, if that's what it even was. It wasn't rational. It wasn't... I didn't even know what it was.

It was stupid, that's what it was.

Lawson gave me a nervous smile. "I know Charlie would think it was me doing him a favour by coming all this way, but I can assure you, the contrary is true. Thank you for inviting us into your home with your family, and thank you for allowing me the opportunity to study these butterflies. I'm truly grateful." He never broke eye contact and he was strangely intense, even though he clearly had no clue how he came across. "But if you don't mind, I'd like to call it a day."

"Not at all. Might wanna set your alarm for five."

Lawson gave a nod and left me feeling even worse. There I was thinkin' resentful thoughts about Jack, and Lawson was nothing but polite and thankful. Charlie walked in, took one look at me, and took my hand. He led me out, turning the lights off as he went. Jack must have gone to bed too, because the house was dark except for a line of light from under their bedroom door. Charlie didn't stop, though. He walked me into our room and closed the door behind me.

"Trav, what's wrong?"

I almost laughed. There weren't no point in denying anything. He knew me too well. "It's stupid."

"Nothin's stupid if it's how you feel." His eyes were imploring, searching mine for answers. "Talk to me."

"I keep thinking of you being with him."

Charlie's eyes went wide. "With Jack? What happened to the Travis tellin' me 'It's my ring on your finger and I know damn well who you belong to.'?"

"That was before he was here. And before he was a real person. A good-looking, real person, I might add." I sighed. "He's been with you. He's touched you, tasted you. He's heard the way you whimper and seen how your eyes roll closed when you come."

He blinked.

"It's stupid and I don't like feeling like this, but I can't help it. I thought I'd be okay with it. I *was* okay with it. Until I saw him. Then he was a real person."

Charlie put his hand to my face. "It was a long time ago. I can't change my history." Then he leaned in all close, took a breath and nudged his nose to mine, giving me an almost kiss. He murmured, "But Trav, if he's one grain of sand, then you're the entire fucking desert."

I tried not to smile and failed. I leaned into his hand. "Thank you. And I dunno why I feel like this."

He leaned against me, pushing me against the door, and kissed my neck up to my ear. "Because the way I whimper when you're buried inside me is just for you. And if I roll my eyes closed when you make me come, it's because you make me. Not anyone else. Never anyone else."

I ran my hands over his ass and pulled our hips closer, grinding our erections together through our jeans. "Charlie."

He slid his hand between us and palmed my dick. He spoke against my lips. "Wanna hear me whimper, Travis?"

I kissed him and pushed him toward the bed. The backs of his legs hit the frame, and I turned him around, fixin' to kiss the back of his neck and grind my hard-on against his ass. Reaching around, I undid his belt. He raised his hips for me. "Fuck yes."

I hummed and undid his jeans, slipping my hand inside and gripping his cock through his briefs. I shucked his jeans down over his hips, then pulled his underpants down to his thighs. I bit down on his neck as I wrapped my hand around his length and pressed my erection against his ass crack. Charlie let his head fall back onto my shoulder and he moaned. "Trav. Please."

"Get on the bed." I stepped back, giving him room to turn around and sit down, and by the time I'd grabbed the lube, he had his boots off and was tugging at his jeans. I grabbed the denim and pulled them off his legs. He grinned and did away with his undies and threw his shirt across the room.

I toed out of my boots, watchin' as he got himself comfortable, lying back with his head on the pillows and his legs spread wide, giving his own cock a slow pull. I was gonna take my time, maybe tease him a little, but then he licked his lips. "Trav." He took the bottle of lube and slicked his fingers, then slipped his hand down between his legs. He groaned when he fingered himself.

I stripped in a flash and quickly found myself on my knees, between his thighs. I watched as he fucked his own fingers until I couldn't bear it. "Take your hand away."

He did as I said but used his slicked fingers to coat my cock, pumping me and positioning me against his hole. "Just do it, Trav. You want me to whimper, then fucking make me whimper."

I pushed against him, that brief resistance giving way until I slid inside him. His eyes went wide and his mouth fell open and a whining sound escaped him, so I leaned over him and covered his mouth with mine.

And whimper he did. That glorious sound he made with every thrust, with every slide of my cock inside him, reachin' deeper and deeper. Part of me wanted to shush him; part of me wanted Jack to hear him.

Charlie gripped my ass, urging me to go faster, harder, until my orgasm crashed over me and I came inside him. I crumpled on top of him, too caught up in my own pleasure, my own head, to consider Charlie.

And he wasn't havin' none of that. He rolled us over

and pushed me onto my stomach. I was face down on the bed, and he got to his knees and grabbed the lube. I knew what he was about to do.

I wanted it.

I lifted my ass and stretched my spine, relishing in the warm buzz of pleasure still flowin' through my veins. Charlie straddled my thighs, poured cool lube down my crack, then pressed his cock against my willing hole. And he pushed in. No preparation, no stretching.

Just how I liked it.

When he was fully buried inside me, he gave me a second to adjust, then put his lips to my ear. "As I belong to you, you belong to me."

He pulled out and slammed back in. I couldn't explain the noises that escaped me. The grunts, the pleading. He fucked me like he owned me, and in many ways he did. In every way, he did.

And with a final thrust, he filled me completely and spilled inside me. Shuddering and jerking as his orgasm took hold of him. He collapsed onto my back, kissing my neck. He nuzzled his nose into my nape. "Shower?"

"Yeah."

Now if Jack and Lawson hadn't heard us in the bedroom, surely they had to hear laughing in the bathroom.

CHAPTER SIX

LAWSON

THE RIDE OUT to where the butterflies were was as long and bumpy as it was beautiful. Charlie had explained that we were to follow them. Our convoy of two vehicles would head east toward the neighbour's property. He explained they normally flew the helicopter over, but with this many people, it couldn't happen. Strangely enough, I didn't mind the drive.

I'd always thought myself to be more of a mountains guy or even partial to the ocean. I'd never even considered the desert to be anything but heat, dust, and flies, but there was a beauty here that I couldn't find words for.

I doubted I'd survive a summer here, though, and I was grateful for the cool morning. After an age, we came to a fence line. It ran like a rickety spine up the scorched red back of this land. Land that baffled me as to how anything survived out here. How Charlie and Travis ever farmed this dirt was a mystery to me.

We followed the fence north for a while, until a four-wheel drive came into view on the other side of the fence. I saw, then, a man who stood by his vehicle, next to an open gate. Charlie drove through, we followed, and we both came to a stop.

"This must be Greg," Jack mused, shutting down the engine. He was mid-forties, maybe, with blond-grey hair. Charlie and Travis were already out and shaking hands with him, their friendship evident by their smiles. Jack and I got out of the Defender. The autumn heat here was as hot as a summer day back home.

Greg greeted us with a warm handshake and the kind of smile I was starting to think was an Outback thing. "Welcome to Queensland," Greg said, "where the good folk live. Not like them Territorians." He gave a pointed nod to Travis and Charlie with a good-natured grin. "Thank you both so much for coming."

"It's no problem at all," I reassured him. "I'm excited to see these butterflies. I hope they are what I think they are."

Greg gave me a hard nod. "Me too. Charlie tell ya 'bout the pipeline they wanna run through here?"

"He did, yes." I understood why I was here, without any doubt. They'd been very honest about it from the start. Their interest was not in the butterfly like mine was. Their interest in the butterfly was in hope it might stop the government staking a claim on Greg's land. I cared not for motive. I had my eyes set on the finish line, and that was to find a butterfly in a country it shouldn't be found in. I smiled at Greg and clapped my hands together. "So, if we'd not like to waste anymore time, let's go find them."

Greg grinned at me. "I like you already, son."

We each took our respective vehicles in a convoy further northeast into Greg's property. There was still red dirt as far as the eye could see, but there were more patches of greenery, thickets of khaki against the red under the bluest sky I think I might have ever seen.

"It's very beautiful, isn't it?" Jack asked, breaking the silence.

"I was just thinking that very thing." I gave him a smile. "I'm getting excited about what we might find today."

Jack laughed. "I can tell. You're doing that knee-bouncing thing."

I tried to keep my leg still. "I am concerned, though. What if it's not what we're hoping to find? That is, what will become of Greg's farm?"

Jack reached over the console and took my hand. "Whatever we find today is not your responsibility. If it's not the African butterfly, then there's nothing you can do to change that. You're here to simply identify, catalogue, and report."

I took comfort from the gentle squeeze of his fingers and went back to watching the landscape.

Finally, we came to a stop in front of a line of trees atop a bit of ridgeline. There were eucalypt trees, but also the *Grewia insularis*. It was a smallish treelike shrub with yellow flowers that I'd only seen in photographs. Finding that plant spiked my excitement because it was the only plant the White-barred Emperor laid its eggs upon and a favoured plant of the caterpillar to eat. It was also a signifi-cant find in its own right. That nervous excitement was now becoming a full-body, jittery feeling.

"Wow," I said, walking over to the edge of the ridge, which I could now see was a creek bank. If it could be called a creek. There was barely enough water in it to constitute a trickle.

I didn't realise Charlie, Travis, and Greg were standing beside me until Charlie spoke. "What's wow?"

I took a leaf of the *Grewia insularis* between my fore-finger and thumb, rubbing it, then smelling the oily residue it left on my skin. "This plant," I started, then turned to look for Jack. He was pulling my research tubs from the back of the four-wheel drive. "I'll need Jack to verify—he's the botanical one—but I do believe this plant is a new find. In Australia, anyway."

"This plant?" Greg asked. "It runs north, right along this creek for miles."

"Well, if it is the *Grewia insularis*, it's only typically found in Africa and on Christmas Island. What it's doing here in the middle of the Australian Outback, is anyone's guess."

"But it'd explain why an African butterfly would be found here, though, wouldn't it?" Travis asked.

I nodded. "Indeed, it would." Their smiles became grins, so I added, "But let's not get ahead of ourselves just yet."

Jack walked over to the shade of the gum tree and put the tubs down in the dirt. He pulled the lid off the top one, fished out my digital barometric reader, and handed it to me. We'd done this together so many times now, we had it down to an art. I took my usual readings and made notes while Jack started in on the plant. He photographed, measured, documented, took foliage samples, flowers and fruits included. While he sat himself in the shade and referenced the plant with known botanical sites online, I went about searching for a butterfly. Crouching down to inspect the underside of the foliage, I checked the closest shrub for evidence. I found some old egg casings, which I collected, and there was evidence of chrysalises, but no butterfly.

I stood up and looked down the embankment. It was a mix of shale and red dirt, only four feet deep at this point. The water was just a few inches deep and maybe a metre wide.

Charlie, Travis, and Greg left us alone to do our work, mostly. "You can walk down the embankment," Charlie said. "It gets steeper further north. Becomes more of a rock face, but you can get down here easy enough. Those plants are down there too."

He was right. The bank was easy to climb down where we'd parked our vehicles, and I could see the ridgeline was taller further off in the distance, rising up several metres from the creek below it. "How far did you say this creek ran?" I asked Greg.

"About fifty miles or so. It's spring-fed from the Artesian Basin."

"And these plants are found right along that distance?"

He nodded. "Pretty sure it's them. The cattle don't touch 'em, so I never paid much attention to 'em, to be honest."

I picked up the three research tubs and called out to Jack to let him know where I was going. "Jack, I'm heading north up the creek."

He put the iPad down. "I'll come with you. I'm still waiting for an official ID on the plant. Don't know how long it will take."

I jumped down the small ledge and waited for Jack to join me. He took the two top tubs from me, and we walked further up the creek bed with the others following not far behind us. It was maybe half a kilometre up when I stopped. I put the tub into the sand and took out my camera. The creek was a little wider here but still only a few inches deep, so I simply walked to the other side. The embankment was steep, a geographical timeline spanning a million years in lines of red shale and sand. But there were also shrubs dotted along the cracks, fed by the creek.

I crouched down to inspect the underside of the leaves

and found what I was looking for. A caterpillar. Chrysalis casings, more caterpillars. I took a run of photographs and must have disturbed a branch at just the right time because there was a flutter of brown and white, and I was suddenly face-to-face with a butterfly.

About a six-centimetre wingspan, with a very distinct white bar across its hindwing, copper-brown and black scales. It was beautiful.

It was also a *Charaxes brutus.*

I was certain.

I stood up and grinned at Jack, who was standing with the others just a few metres away on the other side of the creek. Charlie looked at me, then at him and asked, "What does that look mean?"

Jack laughed. "Well, Lawson only smiles like that for two reasons: me or butterflies."

"He found it?" Travis asked excitedly. "It's the African one?"

I nodded. "I found it." Then I amended. "Well, I'm almost certain. But I'll need to send the photos for verification. Get samples and take some specimen, if I can." I looked at Jack. "Would you mind getting the bag of spoilt fruit from the back of the four-wheel drive?"

"I'll grab it," Travis said, already turning and jogging back the way we'd come.

Jack opened the research tubs and took out specimen jars. He leapt the small creek easily and helped me collect egg casings and an empty chrysalis. Travis came back and set the bag down, as I instructed. "Rip it open and let the fruit spread out like a banquet."

Twenty minutes later, while Jack and I were still busy documenting what we'd collected, Charlie called out, "Uh, guys?"

I looked over to him to find all three men facing the bag of ruined fruit. Like vultures to a carcase, the White-barred Emperor had come. There were over a dozen, maybe more. Fast and fluttering, they flew seemingly without purpose, skipping on the air, but were zoning in on the fruit. I could see why Travis first thought they were small birds.

I grabbed the camera and splashed into the water, quickly snapping as many photographs as I could, zooming in for every minute detail. Jack slowly edged in, and without disturbing them, he picked up half a browned peach and smeared the juice and softened flesh on his hand. Then he just stood there with his hand outstretched and waited.

It didn't take long. One butterfly flittered over to him, settling on his finger. Jack's grin widened as the butterfly began drinking from his skin with its proboscis. "This never gets old," he said with a look of wonder.

And I would never tire of seeing him like that. Smiling at the awe of the simplest of things.

I laughed from behind my camera, taking photo after photo.

By this time, an entire kaleidoscope had arrived for the fruit. "Are all butterflies this fast?" Charlie asked, looking up at the sky.

"No, these are one of the fastest butterflies in the world," I explained.

"You sound pretty confident that it's the African butterfly," Travis said.

I lowered my camera and faced him. "There are many things in this world I am wrong about. Butterflies aren't one of them."

Greg's grin grew wider. "So, it is a rare species? Does this mean we can tell the government to shove their pipe where the sun don't shine?"

"There is a process. A lengthy one, I'm sure," I added. "But the sooner I can gather enough evidence, the better."

"What else do we need to do?" Charlie asked. "Aren't some photos enough?"

"I'll send the photos to the National Lepidopterist Society, and I can contact Piers at the Cairns Butterfly Conservatory, and even my old boss, Professor Asterly in Melbourne. I know people who carry weight—"

Jack laughed. "Uh, excuse me, *Doctor* Gale."

"Brighton-Gale," I corrected. It was a kneejerk response.

"Doctor Brighton-Gale," Jack amended. He turned to Charlie, Travis, and Greg. "Don't let his modesty fool you. Lawson here is internationally acclaimed at what he does. If anyone in this country, if not the world, carries weight in lepidoptery, it's him."

I ignored his compliment. "We still need to respect the process. There are boxes that need to be ticked, the appropriate channels—We need to do this correctly so we don't trip over red tape that would impede us further."

"So, what do we need to do?" Charlie asked again.

"Photographic and video evidence is one thing, but a specimen sample would be best."

"A sample?" Jack asked quietly. He brought his hand in front of his face to look at the butterfly on his hand. "As in a dead sample?"

Jack's frown at the thought of killing one of these butterflies made my heart squeeze. I shook my head. "Only as a last resort."

Jack smiled, and Travis clapped his hands together. "Well, Doctor, tell us what evidence we need to get to make this happen."

CHAPTER SEVEN

CHARLIE

YOU KNOW, for a nerdy butterfly guy, a doctor of all butterfly things, he sure could give some orders. "I'll need to document findings for as far as this creek runs. Photos, egg casings, caterpillars, leaf samples, and please, look for any specimen of butterfly that might already be dead."

"It's getting late," Trav said, looking up at the sky. "We got about two hours of daylight left."

I nodded. "Right, then. We'll head north up to as far as these shrubs things are and see what we can find."

"Butterflies aren't nocturnal," Lawson added. "They'll be roosting soon."

"Then we better get going," Trav said.

"You guys right to set up camp? Or you need us to give you a hand?" I asked them.

"Nah, it's fine," Jack said with a smile, putting the lids back on the research tubs. "I'll walk back to the cars with you guys. That way I can get our camp set up while Lawson finishes up down here."

"I should get going back too," Greg said. "What's the plan of attack for tomorrow, then?"

I scrubbed my hand over my face. "If Trav and me drive as far north as this creek runs, take photos and samples, camp there tonight, then do the same on our way back south every so often in the mornin' and Jack and Lawson do the same heading upstream, then we should cover twice the ground, right?"

"Sounds perfect," Lawson said. "I'll send these photographs off tonight, and hopefully by morning we should hear back." Then he turned to Greg. "If these butterflies are determined to be the White-barred Emperor, further field study will be required. Will you have an issue with allowing researchers and ecology specialists on your property?"

"If it stops a massive pipeline runnin' up the guts of my farm, I don't care who has to come out here."

Lawson nodded. "Very good. I've not had any personal experience with how such matters of ecological findings impact governmental infrastructure such as pipelines, though I've read similar cases. There will be reports, environmental studies, flora and fauna impact statements... the list is long."

"And?" Trav asked. "What are you saying?"

"That even if the pipeline is stopped tomorrow, this won't end quickly. These findings and reports can take years to unfold. I'd imagine you'll be on a first-name basis with the Queensland Department of Environmental Sciences and a dozen other ecology specialists in no time."

Greg stared at him. "But in five, ten, fifty years from now, I'll have butterflies on my farm and not a pipeline, right?"

Lawson gave him a smile. "I'd like to hope so."

Greg smiled. "I can live with that."

We left Lawson to watch the butterflies while we all

walked back to our vehicles. I made sure Jack had half the food Ma had given us, half the water, a radio, and a swag. He was already collectin' firewood before we left, and I knew they were competent in the outdoors. So, we said goodbye to Greg, then Trav and I were in the Cruiser and heading north.

We followed the creek as far as we could. Those weird-lookin' shrubs were there, but the ridge had become deeper and it'd take some climbin' down. I was grateful we'd taken the more difficult end of the creek, though. I mighta been okay with Jack and Lawson camping out here, but I was more confident in my and Trav's ability to handle the terrain.

I grabbed Trav's phone for the camera and some of the specimen jars, that looked like the ones the doc made me pee in, and headed for the edge of the bank. "Be careful," Trav said, as he pulled the swag out of the back of the Cruiser, threw it on the ground, and unrolled it.

Careful of my footing, I climbed down the rocky ledge to the creek. The water was deeper here, and as a whole, it wasn't too unlike our lagoon. And that gave me an idea. But first, the butterflies... And there were butterflies here. Not as many, but enough. So I took a bunch of photos of them on the leaves, and because Lawson wasn't there, I shook the branch a little to make the butterflies fly, snapping pics as they did. Then I found some old cocoon things, a caterpillar or two, and as the first-prize trophy, along the rock face, I found a dead butterfly.

Happy with my findings, I climbed back up the ledge and found Trav starting a campfire. I showed him everything I collected and put them in the back of the Cruiser. "Hey, the water looks good down there. Fancy an evenin' swim?"

Trav looked up at me, and a slow-spreadin' smile crept along his face. "I do believe you have bad intentions?"

I chuckled. "That would depend on your definition of bad." He sat down on the swag, and I pounced on him, straddlin' his hips and pushin' him till he was lying on his back. "You know the only thing I find better than a hot and sweaty Travis?"

Trav laughed and his blue eyes shone with somethin' that looked like a whole lotta fun. "A wet Travis?"

I kissed him hard. "Correct."

He grabbed the back of my head and brought me in for another kiss, liftin' his hips a little. "Or you could fuck me right now," he murmured in that give-me-goosebumps way he did. "Skinny dip later."

I crushed my mouth to his and settled my weight on him, my legs between his. He spread his knees wide and rolled his hips, his fingers dug into my scalp, and he bit my lip, making me moan.

But then the radio crackled to life, and I drew my lips away from Travis', half expectin' George's voice to boom through the speaker, checkin' in on us, but it wasn't George. It was Lawson.

"Charlie! Charlie, can you hear me? It's Jack. He's been bitten by a snake."

I WAS UP and off Travis in a heartbeat. Trav threw our gear into the back of the Cruiser while I kicked dirt on the campfire, and we were on our way back literally ten seconds after Lawson's call.

I drove faster than I'd ever driven.

Trav kept tryin' to talk to Lawson, but it was kinda hard

to hear him. All we knew was it was a bite to the hand. He'd been climbin' along some rock face above the creek and stuck his hand on a ledge when he felt a jab on his finger. He'd fallen back in shock but saw the snake. It had a black coloured head and was kinda yellow underneath.

Oh fuck.

Trav looked at me, frowned, and reached for my hand. I took it real quick and threaded our fingers. We both knew what kind of snake that was. And it wasn't good. Inland taipans were the world's deadliest snake.

Jack was conscious. And Lawson couldn't stop crying.

All I could do was squeeze Trav's hand because I knew—I knew in my heart—that if it were Trav layin' down bein' snake bit, I'd be a fucking mess too.

I pressed down on the accelerator, and Travis put a call into the Station. "Ma? Get George. Get him real quick. There's been an accident."

IT WAS ALMOST COMPLETELY dark when their campsite came into view. The fire was out and I knew they'd still be up the creek. So I drove down a bit further and put the Cruiser down over the ridgeline. It was a bit of a shorter drop, but we still bounced in our seats, Trav needed to hold onto the dashboard, but we made it okay. I turned the Cruiser up the creek and floored it again until we saw Lawson kneelin' in the dirt, wavin' at us.

Jack was layin' in front of him, and we both raced over. I could see Lawson had correctly applied a bandage from his fingers to his armpit, and Jack was real still. I was almost scared to ask because it'd been a good forty minutes... Taipans could kill in less time than that.

Then Jack smiled. "Hey."

I dropped to my knees beside him, relief rushin' out with my breath. "Oh, Jesus. How're you feeling?"

Jack blinked real slow. "My hand hurts."

"Headache? Nausea? Dizziness?" Travis pressed.

"Nope."

Lawson sniffled. He was holding Jack's other hand, and I realised then that his eyes were red and he looked real pale. "He says he feels okay, but we're in the middle of nowhere. We're so far from help, it wouldn't matter anyway." His bottom lip trembled.

I put my hand on his shoulder. "I radioed for George. He's bringin' the chopper in now. Should be here any minute. He'll take him to hospital."

Tears fell down Lawson's cheeks, and he sobbed. "Thank you."

"Lawson," I said gently. "It sounds like an inland taipan, and I gotta tell ya, that's not good. But the fact he's not dead yet is a real good sign."

Lawson's teary gaze shot to mine. "What?"

"If it was a bite to kill, he'd already be dead or in so much pain he'd wish he was. The fact that he's okay tells me it was a dry bite. A warning bite. The snake was probably sleepin'. Jack still needs to get to a hospital, though, just to be sure. You did everything right. You kept him still. The bandage looks good."

Travis put his hand on Jack's chest. "You still feeling okay?"

Jack gave a small nod. "Yeah. More worried about Lawson."

Lawson laughed through his tears. "Usually it's me that needs saving." He put Jack's hand to his lips and kissed it, then cried some more.

"Can tell you what, though," Jack said soothingly, looking above our heads. "I've never seen a night sky look anything like this."

We all looked upwards. The Outback sky was putting on a show, that was for sure. And I guess with Jack being on his back looking up at it, it was hard not to marvel at her. She was a blanket of stars, of galaxies, that weren't nothing short of spectacular.

"Ya know," I said, figurin' he was trying to placate Lawson some. "I've seen thousands of night skies out here, and it still amazes me every time."

Jack smiled at Lawson, and Lawson leaned down and kissed him on the lips. "Trust you to be too busy to die because you're looking at the sky."

We all laughed in a relieved kinda way, and then we heard it. A far off helicopter getting closer until we saw the spotlight. "George can't land down here. We need to get Jack back to camp without moving him too much," I explained. "So, we're gonna lift you into the Cruiser then drive you out, okay?"

Jack nodded, so Trav and I both lifted him up, and Lawson quickly ran to open the door. We lifted him inside and Lawson scrambled in after him. I reversed the whole way down the creek until the bank was small enough for the Cruiser to make it up. The last thing I wanted to do was roll it and see us all end up in hospital. By the time we got out, George had the chopper down, the rotors slowin' to a stop, and he was out of the cockpit waitin' for us.

"I can walk to the helicopter," Jack said.

"No you won't," I said, puttin' an arm around him, helping him out of the seat. "You need to keep your heart rate down."

Trav and I carried Jack in more of a sitting-up position

to the helicopter. It was kinda awkward going, but we got him there. Lawson stood back, his eyes filled with water. "I can't go with him," he mumbled. The helicopter was only big enough for the pilot and one passenger.

"We'll follow you," I told George, knowing Lawson would hear.

George started the chopper and the rotors began to spin. I grabbed Lawson, but he shook off my hand and ran over to Jack, grabbed his face, and planted a kiss on his lips. Trav raced in and grabbed Lawson's arm, pullin' him back so George could get the chopper off the ground. Dust swirled and bit our faces and we had to shield our eyes, then by the time the air had settled around us, so had the darkness. And that too-loud silence.

Lawson just stood there. Not knowin' what else to say, I put my hand on his shoulder. "Come on. Let's get packed up and go."

Fresh tears fell down his cheeks, and he looked so utterly, horribly lost. But he nodded, and five minutes later, he had his research tubs squared away, Trav rolled up the swag, I collected the water and food, and we headed home.

I drove Lawson's Defender, knowin' his wits were far from with him, and Trav followed in the Cruiser.

Lawson was quiet a while, lookin' out at the darkness. "I'm sorry I lost it back there," he said, breakin' the silence.

"Nah, that's all right. If it were me, and Travis was lyin' there like that, I'da done more than lose my shit."

He nodded and went back to starin' out the window, and I had to wonder if he was crying some more. He gave himself some time before he spoke again. "You know, a few years back, I almost died from cane toad poisoning. We were in the tropical rainforest of North Queensland and it was pouring rain... Anyway, he carried me on his back, in the dark, and walked me to meet an ambulance. He must have carried me for a kilometre or more, through some slippery and rugged terrain." He swallowed hard. "He saved my life."

"And tonight you saved his."

The look on his face told me he didn't believe that. He surprised me by barking out a laugh. "There is a long-running joke in our families that I'm the one who constantly needs saving. They'll never believe me because he's always the strong one; there's nothing he can't do." He frowned, and his voice went real quiet. "I can't even think about what would happen if..."

"I'm sure he's okay," I said, though I had no real idea of knowin'. "Like I said, if it was a taipan and a full-venom bite, he wouldn't be sittin' up in a helicopter right now."

Lawson nodded, but it was a hollow acknowledgement. I didn't blame him none. Because if it was Trav in Jack's shoes right now, I wouldn't believe what anyone told me until I saw him with my own eyes. Lawson's mind must've been goin' down the same track as mine. "Where's George taking him?"

"Home first. He'll need to refuel. Then to Alice Hospital."

He nodded slowly. "I hope you don't think it rude of me to follow him tonight. When we get back to your house, I'll be leaving as soon as I'm packed. I don't mean to offend your hospitality—"

"I get it, Lawson. And I'm not offended. If it were Travis... well, I wouldn't be anywhere else either."

He gave me a bit of a smile. "Thank you."

I was just about to ask where this left the whole butterfly thing when the CB radio cracked to life. It was

George. "Hey Charlie," he said, his slow drawl a familiar welcome. "Everything okay?"

Instinctively, I checked my rear vision mirror to check on Trav's headlights not too far behind us. "Yeah. All good here. You refuelling?"

"Well, I was, but our patient here says he's well enough to stay."

"He what?" Lawson asked.

"Lawson," George drawled. "Thought you might want to speak some sense into him, son."

I handed the radio mouthpiece to Lawson, and his jaw set. "Jack? Have you lost your mind?"

There was a ruffling sound, a muffled voice, then Jack's voice came on the radio. "Lawson, I'm okay."

"Do you have a degree in neurotoxicology that I'm unaware of?"

Jack snorted. "No."

"Then why won't you go to hospital?"

There was silence so long that Lawson looked at the mouthpiece like it was a phone with a screen. "Because I won't go without you."

Lawson let the hand holding the radio mouthpiece fall into his lap and he put his thumb and forefinger into his eyes, I realised, to stem his tears. "How long until we get back to your house?" he asked me quietly.

"Hour and a half."

He spoke into the radio. "I'm ninety minutes away. And I'll drive you to the hospital myself."

"Lawson, I feel okay. My hand hurts and my arm aches, but I have no other symptoms."

"Then you'll have no problems in letting the good medical doctors of the local hospital assess you."

"See you soon, Lawson."

The radio clicked off, and Lawson smiled, clearly more relieved in hearing Jack's voice and that he was okay. "Stubborn man."

The drive was silent after that, which was just as well. Driving out here durin' the day was hard enough; driving at night was a whole new world of worry. There was no road, as such, but the track to Greg's place from mine was worn well enough that we could see it, but it took all my concentration. I kept an eye on Travis' headlights in my rear-vision mirror, makin' sure he wasn't too far behind us. I radioed him to tell him what was going on and how George was grounded for a bit—and just to hear his voice—and soon enough, the homestead came into view.

George met us out front, and I had a fair guess that wherever Jack was, Ma was keeping him company. Lawson rushed inside, and I followed him. Jack was on the sofa, and sure enough, Ma was on the recliner watchin' him like a hawk. Lawson quickly sat beside him, needin' to touch his face. With better lighting, the bandage wrapped tight around his arm looked worse than before, and he looked pale as hell. I heard Travis pull up outside, followed by his boots on the veranda steps. That screen door openin' had never sounded so good.

He was quick to slide his arm around my waist and plant his lips to my temple. "How's the patient?"

I gently tapped Travis' chest. "I'm gonna get the hospital on the phone. See what they reckon."

He hadn't taken his eyes off Jack. "Good idea."

Lawson stood up and looked right at me. "I'd appreciate it very much if you could tell them to expect us in about three hours. We're leaving."

"Lawson—" Jack started to protest, but Lawson spun to give him a look of fire and determination. I'm pretty sure

Travis used the same one on me, and there weren't no point in arguin' with it. Just no point at all.

Ma nodded wisely. "I'll help you pack, dear."

When they'd left the room, I grabbed the phone, and when I came back out, I found Trav'd sat down beside Jack. "You feelin' okay?" he asked him.

He nodded. "Yeah. But Lawson's right."

I had to agree. "Yes, he is."

Travis laughed. "One person in every couple always is."

I chuckled at that and Jack snorted, but his smile faded away. He looked right at Travis. "Thank you for having us out here. It's a beautiful place. Beautiful home, family."

Trav just gave him a knowin' smile. "I wouldn't trade it for the world."

I got through to the hospital, so I left Trav with Jack and went back out to the Cruiser while I explained down the phone what had happened and how they were on their way into emergency now. I had those samples Lawson wanted, and when I clicked off the phone call and collected all the specimen jars, Lawson came out with the first bag.

"Where's my car?" Lawson asked, looking completely baffled.

I almost laughed. "George's fuellin' it up for ya."

He put his bag on the veranda. "Oh. I hadn't even thought of that. You have your own fuel tanks here?"

"Have to." I handed him the specimen jars. "Got everything you asked for. And found a dead butterfly, so I grabbed it too."

"Thank you." He sighed, long and loud. "I will forward everything I have onto the appropriate experts first thing. I can imagine there'll be plenty of waiting time at the hospital."

I nodded slowly. "I truly do appreciate you comin' all

this way. And I'm sorry it ended like this. He'll be fine, I'm sure of it."

George drove their rental up to the house, and I opened up the back tailgate. Lawson put the specimen jars into one of his tubs, and I grabbed their bags. By the time I'd thrown them into the back, Travis appeared at the door with Jack. "I offered to carry him," Trav said, "but he declined."

Jack laughed, but he was clearly tired and walkin' like he'd rather not be upright. He held his bandaged arm out awkwardly, and he still didn't have much colour. He made it down the steps, and Lawson got him buckled into the front passenger seat. Lawson turned to us all. "Thank you again."

I waved him off. "Drive safe. Watch for roos."

"And emus," Travis added.

"And camels," George said.

Then Ma threw in, "And road trains."

Lawson's eyes widened with each one, and I'm pretty sure he mumbled something about never leaving Tasmania again, got in behind the wheel, and we watched them drive away.

The four of us stood in silence on the veranda, watching the red tail lights disappear down the driveway.

"Think he'll be all right?" Trav asked.

"Sure he will," George said. "If he ain't dead yet..."

We all nodded, but none of us made a move for inside.

"You boys want a cup of tea before bed?" Ma asked.

"Nah," I answered. "How was Milly tonight? Not too much trouble?"

"She's an angel," Ma said. Which was true, if angels were cute as they were stubborn and could swap out their halos for horns any time they wanted.

I sighed, still lookin' up at the stars. "The sky sure is pretty tonight."

The four of us stood there, all lookin' upwards. George hummed and put his arm around Ma's shoulder. "Always is."

Travis hung his arm around my neck and kissed the side of my head. "Always."

CHAPTER EIGHT

JACK

I WOKE up in hospital to find a sleeping Lawson in a chair beside the bed. It was daytime out the window, there were bandages up my forearm, and whatever drugs they'd given me took away the pain.

And sweet Jesus there had been pain.

I'd tried not to let on too much because I didn't want Lawson to worry any more than he already was. In the creek bed, when it first happened and he was strapping my arm, he was certain I was going to die. He was a fucking mess.

And maybe it was foolish of me to not get to the hospital sooner, but I just couldn't leave him. I didn't want to go without him, as much as I didn't want him out all those miles away without me. God, he was so upset in that creek bed...

I knew I had to do whatever it took to never put him through that again, but when we'd arrived at the hospital, the doctor had asked me to rate my pain from one to ten. I couldn't lie, so I'd said it was a nine. When he asked me to describe it, I said it was kinda like someone hit my hand with a sledgehammer, then poured acid over it while stabbing it with an ice pick.

He stared at me and asked what could possibly be added to make it a ten out of ten because that sounded as unbearable as it could get. My answer was simple. "If it had happened to my husband and I had to watch. That'd be a ten."

Lawson started to cry when I said that, but a nurse put her arm around him and they wheeled me away. They gave me something for the pain and it made me sleepy, but I do remember seeing my hand when they'd inspected the wound, and I remembered them taking me to a room for observation.

Which is where I woke up. I found myself just watching Lawson for a minute. He was sound asleep in one of those ungodly uncomfortable chairs, and I wished like hell he could climb up onto the bed with me.

Watching him wasn't too bad either, though. And as if he could feel my eyes on him, he stirred awake. "Jack," he said, sliding forward in his chair. He took my hand. "I was so worried. How are you feeling?"

"I feel good."

"They've given you pain relief."

"I'm hungry."

"Shall I go and find out what you can eat?"

"Yes, please."

He stood and planted a kiss on my forehead. "Won't be long."

I must have dozed off while I waited, because I woke up again to the sound of voices. Lawson, of course, and some other voices I recognised. Charlie and Travis, and Milly too.

"Hey," I said, trying to sit up.

Lawson fixed my bed so I was more upright, and Charlie gave me a huge grin. "Didn't mean to wake ya."

"No, it's fine. I must have dozed off again." I shook my head a little, trying to clear it, and Lawson took my good hand. "What time is it?"

"Ten," Charlie answered. "We just got here. Thought we'd come and see how you were."

"And Daddy said we can get me some ice cream," Milly piped up with. Her eyes were big and brown, and her red curls were gorgeous.

Travis grinned and scooped her up and sat her on his hip. "And Dada. Because Dada lurves ice cream," he said. Milly laughed then, and she clung to him. She was wearing a blue tutu, brown boots, and a Dallas football shirt. She really was equal parts her fathers' daughter.

Lawson was looking at them with a happy sadness I'd never seen on him before. It was a look that never quite went away the whole time Charlie, Travis, and Milly were there, even when he was explaining he'd heard back from the Australian Lepidoptery Society, who had confirmed from the photos and video evidence the butterfly was indeed the African White-barred Emperor.

The plant had been confirmed, also, from my request, and the Fauna Conservation of Queensland was extremely interested.

"I'd imagine I'll know more within forty-eight hours. As I explained to Greg, the stay on the pipeline might be immediate, pending reviews and reports, but the long-term process can take years."

"So, it's all good?" Charlie asked excitedly.

"Do you remember the bell frog that almost stopped the Sydney Olympics?" Lawson asked.

Charlie and Travis both shook their heads. "Nope."

Lawson explained, "The government was all set to develop a large area of disused land near the Olympic centre until they found a rare frog. There were ecological studies done to the nth degree, as you could very well imagine. But they won. A new location was found; the frog and its habitat remains."

"So if a little frog can stop the freakin' Olympics, then we stand a chance, right?" Charlie pressed on, clearly trying not to sound too hopeful.

Lawson nodded in a so-so manner and gave him a tired smile. "I certainly hope so. I'll let you know as soon as I hear so Greg can start the paperwork and legal proceedings. I'd hazard a guess there will be a lot of it."

"That's real good news," I said. "I'm glad it worked out."

"I'm sorry you're in here, though," Charlie added. "But it was real good to see you again, Jack. Maybe next time we can come down to Tassie?"

"Fly fishing?" Travis asked, his eyes almost as wide as his grin.

"Definitely," Lawson answered. "You're most welcome anytime. I don't think we'll be leaving for any more butterfly expeditions in a hurry."

I snorted. "Until you get asked."

"Maybe not even then," he said, and that sad smile was back. "I think I'll stay homebound for a while."

Charlie, Travis, and Milly stayed for just a few more minutes before the lure of ice cream became too much for Milly. With fond farewells, they left, and Lawson wheeled the table over. "You must be starving. You're allowed a light meal, so I got you a sandwich and some fruit, and juice and water."

He unwrapped everything for me because of my

bandaged hand, and I devoured it all. "Have you eaten?" I asked him around my last mouthful of food.

"Yes, earlier. I'll grab some lunch soon and get you something else as well."

He was still quiet, sad even. I held out my good hand and waited for him to take it. "Want to tell me what's wrong?"

"Only you almost dying."

"Pretty scary, huh?" I joked. "I remember when it was you in the hospital bed almost dying. Took ten years off me, so I know you've had a rough night. I'm sorry."

He squeezed my hand. "I wasn't joking about not leaving for any more expeditions. I'm done, honestly. There's enough work with my Tillman Copper, and I'm sure there's more academia I can contribute to—"

"Want to tell me what's really wrong?" I interrupted. I knew him. I *knew* him, and there was something he wasn't telling me.

He frowned and his eyes became glassy. "I don't think now is the right time to bring it up. When you're home and well, we can talk about it."

"Lawson, please just tell me. Something's bothering you, and I can't stand not knowing what it is."

"If I tell you, I don't want you to answer. Not yet. I want you to think it over for the time it deserves."

"Lawson," I urged.

His bottom lip began to quiver, and I worried I might not like what he was about to say.

"I want a child."

I blinked.

"I want what Charlie and Travis have. Their very own child. I never thought about it before now. It wasn't anything I ever considered... I didn't know I wanted it until

I saw them. They're a family. I want that with you. I don't know how to make it happen or if you even want that, but I do, Jack, I want that. I think we'd be pretty good fathers. Well, you would be. I started to picture it, you know, which wasn't helpful at all, because I could see you working on the gardens and a little boy in gumboots, just like you, trudging behind you, copying everything you do, and Jack, so help me God, I've never wanted anything more in my life."

I was stunned.

He frowned. "You don't have to say anything right now, and I told you this wasn't the best time or place, and I do realise I've just dropped a rather monumental bombshell, but if you'd just consider it. I was thinking adoption, if you agree, of course. Just give it time to get used to the idea, the possibility even."

"No."

His eyes shot to mine. Hurt and sorrow became instant tears. "You won't even think about it?"

"No. I don't need to think about it," I said, squeezing his hand and fighting a smile. "I think that's a bombshell I'd like to explore. Being a family with you."

His tears fell down his cheeks; but his whole face lit up. "You do?"

I nodded. "You're wrong about one thing, though. The little boy who's following me around the backyard would wear gumboots *and* a bow tie."

Lawson laughed, then got to his feet. He cupped my face and kissed me hard on the mouth. Then he wiped the tears from his cheeks, turned, and headed for the door. "We need to leave. We need to go home. Right now."

I laughed as he went in search of someone to discharge me, impatient as ever. I let my head fall back on the pillow and sighed to the empty room. If we thought our lives had changed when we met each other, when we married, that was nothing compared to how our lives were about to change. Did I want a family with Lawson? Did I want to become a dad like Charlie and Travis? You bet your life I did.

If imago was singular and imagines was two, I made a mental note to ask Lawson if there was an entomological term for imago times three.

I KICKED the dust off my boots on the veranda steps and put my hat on the hook inside the door, just like always. I found Milly, Nugget, and Trav on the couch. She was readin' them a book, and they all looked up at me and smiled. Yep. All of 'em.

"Can I get you two a drink or somethin'?"

"Juice please, Dada," Milly answered.

Travis held up two fingers. "Two, please."

I wandered into the kitchen and found Ma at the sink. I grabbed two glasses and a plastic My Little Pony tumbler from the overhead cupboard and gave Ma a kiss on the cheek. "Need a hand with anything?"

"No, love. Nara's just grabbing me some veggies from the garden."

I grabbed the juice, poured the three drinks, and put the bottle back in the fridge. "Trav's having a lesson on *Green Eggs and Ham*. I better go save him."

Ma smiled contentedly. "Oh, I popped the mail on your desk."

"Thanks," I said, leavin' her to it. "I'll grab it." After I'd handed the drinks out and put mine beside the sofa, I collected the mail to open and sort through while Milly did her reading. I almost sat on Nugget, then had to wrestle with him so he didn't eat the mail. There were bills and statements and the usual crap, but the letter on the bottom was handwritten. The envelope was thick, quality stuff, as was the paper inside it.

It was an invitation with a photo on it. And I knew who it was from before I even read it. Because the photo was of a little boy, maybe a year old, cute as freakin' hell with his little fancy suspenders, long-sleeve shirt, and a bow tie. There could be only one couple I knew who'd dress their kid in a bow tie.

Charlie, Travis, & Milly
You're invited to celebrate the first birthday of Brennan Brighton-Gale.

"Trav?" I said with a smile.

"Yeah?"

I held up the invitation. "About that trip to Tasmania...?"

Trav's whole face lit up, then he melted. "Oh, I'm so glad it came through for them."

We knew from Jack and Lawson's last trip to Greg's farm that they were in the middle of the adoption process. They'd told us it was their time here, seein' me, Trav, and Milly, made them realise bein' a family was a possibility. Which apparently had now become a reality.

"He's wearing a bow tie." I gave Trav a smile, then looked back at the photo. Brennan had real chubby cheeks, dark brown eyes, and the cheekiest grin. "He's a real cute kid."

Trav gave me a look that made my heart beat itself all outta rhythm. "We should go. To Tasmania for the party. For them."

"We should." I tickled Milly. "Wanna go on a plane trip?"

She nodded excitedly. "Yes! Can Nugget come?"

I shook my head. "No."

She pouted and Nugget stared at me with his little mouth open like he couldn't believe it. I tried not to smile. "But there'll be butterflies. And we might find a Tasmanian devil."

Milly's eyes went wide. "Can I have one?" Even Nugget bounced on her lap like he was all excited.

Travis and I both laughed, then answered resoundingly and in unison. "No!"

~ The End ~

ABOUT THE AUTHOR

N.R. Walker is an Australian author, who loves her genre of gay romance. She loves writing and spends far too much time doing it, but wouldn't have it any other way.

She is many things: a mother, a wife, a sister, a writer. She has pretty, pretty boys who live in her head, who don't let her sleep at night unless she gives them life with words.

She likes it when they do dirty, dirty things... but likes it even more when they fall in love. She used to think having people in her head talking to her was weird, until one day she happened across other writers who told her it was normal.

She's been writing ever since...

nrwalker.net

ALSO BY N.R. WALKER

Blind Faith

Through These Eyes (Blind Faith #2)

Blindside: Mark's Story (Blind Faith #3)

Ten in the Bin

Gay Sex Club Stories 1

Gay Sex Club Stories 2

Point of No Return – Turning Point #1

Breaking Point – Turning Point #2

Starting Point – Turning Point #3

Element of Retrofit – Thomas Elkin Series #1

Clarity of Lines – Thomas Elkin Series #2

Sense of Place – Thomas Elkin Series #3

Taxes and TARDIS

Three's Company

Red Dirt Heart

Red Dirt Heart 2

Red Dirt Heart 3

Red Dirt Heart 4

Red Dirt Christmas

Cronin's Key

Cronin's Key II

Cronin's Key III

Cronin's Key IV - Kennard's Story

Exchange of Hearts

The Spencer Cohen Series, Book One

The Spencer Cohen Series, Book Two

The Spencer Cohen Series, Book Three

The Spencer Cohen Series, Yanni's Story

Blood & Milk

The Weight Of It All

A Very Henry Christmas (The Weight of It All 1.5)

Perfect Catch

Switched

Imago

Imagines

Imagoes

Red Dirt Heart Imago

On Davis Row

Finders Keepers

Evolved

Galaxies and Oceans

Private Charter

Nova Praetorian

A Soldier's Wish

Upside Down

The Hate You Drink

Sir

Tallowwood

Reindeer Games

The Dichotomy of Angels

Throwing Hearts

Pieces of You - Missing Pieces #1

Pieces of Me - Missing Pieces #2

Pieces of Us - Missing Pieces #3

Lacuna

Tic-Tac-Mistletoe

Bossy

Code Red

Dearest Milton James

Dearest Malachi Keogh

Christmas Wish List

Code Blue

Davo

The Kite

Learning Curve

Merry Christmas Cupid

To the Moon and Back

Second Chance at First Love

Outrun the Rain

Into the Tempest

Touch the Lightning

EWB - Enemies With Benefits

Holiday Heart Strings

Bloom

The Men from Echo Creek

Titles in Audio:

Cronin's Key

Cronin's Key II

Cronin's Key III

Red Dirt Heart

Red Dirt Heart 2

Red Dirt Heart 3

Red Dirt Heart 4

The Weight Of It All

Switched

Point of No Return

Breaking Point

Starting Point

Spencer Cohen Book One

Spencer Cohen Book Two

Spencer Cohen Book Three

Yanni's Story

On Davis Row

Evolved

Elements of Retrofit

Clarity of Lines

Sense of Place

Blind Faith

Through These Eyes

Blindside

Finders Keepers

Galaxies and Oceans

Nova Praetorian

Upside Down

Sir

Tallowwood

Imago

Throwing Hearts

Sixty Five Hours

Taxes and TARDIS

The Dichotomy of Angels

The Hate You Drink

Pieces of You

Pieces of Me

Pieces of Us

Tic-Tac-Mistletoe

Lacuna

Bossy

Code Red

Learning to Feel

Dearest Milton James

Dearest Malachi Keogh

Three's Company

Christmas Wish List

Code Blue

Davo

The Kite

Learning Curve

Merry Christmas Cupid

To the Moon and Back

Second Chance at First Love

Outrun the Rain

Into the Tempest

Touch the Lightning

EWB

Holiday Heart Strings

Bloom

Series Collections:

Red Dirt Heart Series

Turning Point Series

Thomas Elkin Series

Spencer Cohen Series

Imago Series

Blind Faith Series

Missing Pieces Series

The Storm Boys Series

Free Reads:

Sixty Five Hours

Learning to Feel

His Grandfather's Watch (And The Story of Billy and Hale)

The Twelfth of Never (Blind Faith 3.5)

Twelve Days of Christmas (Sixty Five Hours Christmas)

Best of Both Worlds

Translated Titles:

Italian

Fiducia Cieca (Blind Faith)

Attraverso Questi Occhi (Through These Eyes)

Preso alla Sprovvista (Blindside)

Il giorno del Mai (Blind Faith 3.5)

Cuore di Terra Rossa Serie (Red Dirt Heart Series)

Natale di terra rossa (Red dirt Christmas)

Intervento di Retrofit (Elements of Retrofit)

A Chiare Linee (Clarity of Lines)

Senso D'appartenenza (Sense of Place)

Spencer Cohen Serie (including Yanni's Story)

Punto di non Ritorno (Point of No Return)

Punto di Rottura (Breaking Point)

Punto di Partenza (Starting Point)

Imago (Imago)

Imagines

Il desiderio di un soldato (A Soldier's Wish)

Scambiato (Switched)

Tallowwood

The Hate You Drink

Ho trovato te (Finders Keepers)

Cuori d'argilla (Throwing Hearts)

Galassie e Oceani (Galaxies and Oceans)

Il peso di tut (The Weight of it All)

Pieces of You - Missing Pieces 1

French

Confiance Aveugle (Blind Faith)

A travers ces yeux: Confiance Aveugle 2 (Through These Eyes)

Aveugle: Confiance Aveugle 3 (Blindside)

À Jamais (Blind Faith 3.5)

Cronin's Key Series

Au Coeur de Sutton Station (Red Dirt Heart)

Partir ou rester (Red Dirt Heart 2)

Faire Face (Red Dirt Heart 3)

Trouver sa Place (Red Dirt Heart 4)

Le Poids de Sentiments (The Weight of It All)

Un Noël à la sauce Henry (A Very Henry Christmas)

Une vie à Refaire (Switched)

Evolution (Evolved)

Galaxies & Océans

Qui Trouve, Garde (Finders Keepers)

Sens Dessus Dessous (Upside Down)

La Haine au Fond du Verre (The hate You Drink)

Tallowwood

Spencer Cohen Series

Thomas Elkin One

Lacuna

German

Flammende Erde (Red Dirt Heart)

Lodernde Erde (Red Dirt Heart 2)

Sengende Erde (Red Dirt Heart 3)

Ungezähmte Erde (Red Dirt Heart 4)

Vier Pfoten und ein bisschen Zufall (Finders Keepers)

Ein Kleines bisschen Versuchung (The Weight of It All)

Ein Kleines Bisschen Fur Immer (A Very Henry Christmas)

Weil Leibe uns immer Bliebt (Switched)

Drei Herzen eine Leibe (Three's Company)

Über uns die Sterne, zwischen uns die Liebe (Galaxies and Oceans)

Unnahbares Herz (Blind Faith 1)

Sehendes Herz (Blind Faith 2)

Hoffnungsvolles Herz (Blind Faith 3)

Verträumtes Herz (Blind Faith 3.5)

Thomas Elkin: Verlangen in neuem Design

Thomas Elkin: Leidenschaft in klaren

Thomas Elkin: Vertrauen in bester Lage

Traummann töpfern leicht gemacht (Throwing Hearts)

Sir

So Unendlich Viel Liebe (To the Moon and Back)

Corazón De Tierra Roja 3

Corazón De Tierra Roja 4

ECB (Enemigos con Beneficios)

Floral

Chinese

Blind Faith

Japanese

Bossy

Portuguese

Sessenta e Cinco Horas

www.ingramcontent.com/pod-product-compliance
Lightning Source LLC
Chambersburg PA
CBHW050539190726
48284CB00003B/1137